Flirting With Fate
A Noble Pass Affaire Novella
By
Jerrie Alexander

Acknowledgments

I would be remiss if I didn't acknowledge the following people. Their support, advice, and enthusiasm were invaluable.

To my editors and proofreaders, Brynna Curry, Jena S. O'Connor, Amy Knupp, and Jackie Pressley, your guidance helped me polish this story until it shone. For that, you have my sincere appreciation.

Kym Roberts, you listened to my ideas, poked, and prodded me when the story stalled, and offered encouragement every step of the way. I appreciate you more than I can say.

Last but not least, thanks to my readers. You are why I write. Your emails make my day! I hope you enjoy this story as much as I loved writing it.

Any mistakes are my own!

Dedication

To Jim, my forever love.

"Accept the things to which fate binds you, and love the people with whom fate brings you together, but do so with all your heart."
Marcus Aurelius

One

Elle Reagan's heart pounded against her rib cage, pushing blood through her veins at record speeds. She opened Brandon Ethridge's dresser drawer and surveyed its contents. Careful not to disturb anything, she performed a thorough search. Disappointed to find nothing more than underwear and a collection of silk scarves, she moved to the nightstand next to the bed.

A hand clamped over her mouth, cutting off the scream bubbling up in her throat. An arm slid around her waist and jerked her against a rock-hard chest. She kicked out with her feet and dug her nails into her attacker's wrist.

"Damn it, Elle. Stop that!" The low, gravelly whisper sent her mind spinning. Questions ricocheted through her thoughts.

Logan Ford's voice immobilized her. Elle's fear segued into confusion, making it easy for him to back her across the room. He removed his hand from her mouth and then leaned over until his nose brushed her ear.

"Not a word." His fingers brushed her cheek, sending flashes of heat across her skin.

He opened the French doors and then stepped onto the balcony into the frigid air. Logan pulled her along and stopped when they reached the far corner. He turned her to face him. His expression was as cold as the falling snowflakes.

The sound of a man's voice from inside the suite turned Elle's knees to rubber. She looked up into Logan's dark brown eyes. He'd saved her from being discovered. Questions, such as why he was in Colorado instead of Texas, would have to wait until they were safely off this balcony and out of the horrid weather.

Logan pulled her closer, wrapping his arms around her. His broad back helped shield her from the blizzard. Under different circumstances, she would've enjoyed being inside his strong arms with her head tucked under his chin. Hadn't she daydreamed about him sweeping her off her feet since she'd turned thirteen? Standing outdoors in subzero weather, six floors above the snow-covered ground, made it impossible to enjoy the moment.

He hadn't come for romance, he'd come to interfere.

Elle heard voices rise and fall as people moved through the suite.

"If you pull this deal off, we'll make a fortune," Ethridge's daughter, Nicki, said. "I'm tired of this game."

"A few more days and Liam and Alana will do whatever I recommend," Ethridge said.

Logan's grip tightened, helping Elle forget the weather but not her mission.

"Hurry up. Let's go downstairs." Nicki's tone hinted at impatience. "I want to select the perfect spot for us to stand during the meet-and-greet cocktail party."

Time crawled as Elle and Logan waited until it was safe to go inside. She shivered, regretting not wearing heavier clothes, but then, she hadn't expected to be hiding on a balcony in the snow. She'd planned on finding the evidence she needed and leaving quickly.

Elle had to stop Ethridge. His swindle had to be uncovered and proof sent to the FBI. Maybe then they would act on her grandmother's complaints.

A door slammed. Had someone else entered or had they left? The cold had seeped into her bones to the point of being painful. Logan's head lowered, and his lips brushed her icy ear.

"Stay here until I'm sure it's all clear."

Elle managed a nod and reluctantly released her warm shelter. A minute later, he came back. He dusted snow off them, scooped her into his arms, and carried her inside. Curiosity got the best of her. "What are you doing here?"

"We'll talk later. We have to move. Leaving a trail of wet footprints on the carpet wouldn't be too smart."

In a few long strides, they were out the door and in the hallway. If she hadn't been so pleased to be in his arms, he wouldn't have gotten away with his bossy tone of voice. Logan put her down, took her hand, and they hurried to the elevator. When they were safely inside, he pushed the button marked eight. More questions filled her mind. How did he know her floor number? When was he leaving?

She turned, ready to demand answers, but lost her voice. His hair was damp with melting snow, his shirt was wet and had molded to his chest. Looking down at her, the one man who'd made her speechless for years, smiled. His gaze then conducted a leisurely scan of her body, reminding her that she, too, wore wet clothing.

The elevator doors opened, and without conversation, they walked to her suite. By the time they had entered the common room of her suite, Elle was about to explode. "What the hell are you doing here?"

"Have you lost your mind?" His tone sounded equally full of frustration, which pushed her last hot button.

"What business is it of yours, if I have? And don't answer my question with a question." Did she think he was going to say, *I'm here because I'm crazy about you*? Or that he'd seized this chance to be alone with her? No. She knew exactly who'd sent him. *Damn it, Eric.*

"We're friends. That makes it my business." He leaned against the fireplace mantel, looking right at home and way too sexy.

"Give me a break. We both know why you're here. How is my dear brother?" Logan rushing to Colorado to protect her would've been a dream come true. However, she knew that wasn't the case.

"He's pissed."

"I guess you think I should thank you for saving my butt."

Logan's mouth lifted into a half smile. "You mean for keeping you out of jail? You're welcome."

"You need to go home." Elle stabbed her finger toward the door.

"So do you." He pushed off the mantel. In a couple of long strides, he stood in front of her. "What's with the hair?"

She pulled off the wig and tossed it onto a chair. "Nicki Ethridge is a blonde."

"Jesus." His eyebrows drew together. "I'll go home if you come with me."

"I won this vacation, and I intend to stay right here."

"Bullshit," he said with a shake of his head. "You entered the contest under false pretenses."

"Now you're an expert on what I do and why?" God, he looked good standing there all pissed off.

"I'm smart enough to know you'd never enter a contest to meet some stranger for a possible romantic connection. Give me a fucking break. Somehow, you learned Brandon Ethridge was going to be here. Eric saw through your con weeks ago."

Elle decided to appeal to Logan's sense of fair play. "Don't you dare screw this up for me. I promised Nan I'd either figure out a way to get her money back or gather enough information to put Ethridge in prison."

"You have no idea what you're up against." Logan's jaw muscles twitched, making Elle want to smooth her hand across the stubble on his cheek. "If the FBI can't prove Ethridge is an investment scam artist, what makes you think you can?"

"Because I have a personal interest, and I'm not some branch of the government with other priorities."

"The Feds are working the case, but they need proof. You know...evidence."

"Don't be a smartass." Elle wasn't backing down. His frown relaxed. Had she softened his always-by-the-book approach to life? "I'm asking you not to interfere."

"Let's get you warmed up." He took her hand and led her into her bedroom, stopping at the bed.

Again, Elle had gone speechless. Had she won the argument or been ignored? Exactly what did he have in mind? Whatever it was, her hormones had immediately come to life and were running wild. He'd definitely piqued her interest.

He knelt and looked up at her through thick, dark lashes. "Have a seat."

As if hypnotized, she obeyed. Curiosity had taken control of her brain. He removed her shoes, catching her instep in his hand.

"Your feet are like ice."

Lightning bolts shot up her leg as his fingers kneaded and soothed her foot. Parts of her body instantly warmed and tingled under the pressure of his hands. Parts that shouldn't heat up at his touch. Falling for Logan's Prince Charming routine would be as smart as playing Russian roulette with a fully loaded gun. She'd heard a lot of stories about the broken hearts he'd left in his wake. Self-preservation kicked in, and Elle pulled her foot from his grasp.

"You are not going to stop me. Sending you was a waste of time."

"We'll talk about this after you've had a warm shower and changed into dry clothes."

Logan's audacity brought her out of her hormonal fog. He'd always ordered her around as if he, too, were her brother. "I'm not too cold to listen."

"Shower first." Out came that damn frown. "Want me to help you undress?"

A nervous laugh burst from Elle, embarrassing her. She quickly regained her composure. "Now you're being funny. I'm waiting for you to leave. Go home and tell my brother to mind his own damn business."

Logan's eyes narrowed to slits. He stood and silently left the room, closing the door behind him.

The tension in Elle's neck tightened. No way was Logan leaving. She'd have to come up with a plan to gain his help. He'd have to get his own room. The owners of Castle Alainn had provided her and the male co-winner with a luxurious two-bedroom suite. Each side could be locked off from the rest of the unit, satisfying her wariness of sharing space with a stranger. She couldn't help but worry about what would happen if the guy turned up to find Logan in the common area.

She wasn't concerned that Logan would blow her cover. His loyalty to her brother went back many years. Eric had brought Logan home to play the day after Elle had turned thirteen. She'd immediately developed a crush on him. Not that he'd ever given her a second look. For the next nineteen years, the only physical contact she'd had with Logan was when he'd held her down and scrubbed his knuckles across her head.

Her nerve endings had fired and tingled for all the wrong reasons today. She'd breathed in his scent and felt the strength of his body. The sinking feeling in the pit of her stomach set off warning bells. Logan had no interest in her. He'd proved that in high school by treating her as if she'd had the plague. Still, standing on Ethridge's balcony, staring up at Logan, she'd thought a spark of interest had flared in his eyes. No doubt, it was just concern for her safety.

Shaking off those thoughts, Elle stripped and walked into the bathroom. She turned on the shower, stepped under the warm water, allowing her bones to thaw. She toweled off, dried her hair, and then applied makeup.

Elle slipped on a simple black dress and a pair of heels. She'd blown her budget on clothes for this trip. Her new dress, cut low in the back, accentuated her every curve, but she only gave the mirror a glance. She had to bring Logan over to her side.

She entered the common room to find him standing in front of the fireplace. On the mantel sat two glasses of red wine. His usual unruly shock of black hair had been conquered and combed into place. In typical Logan style, the two-day-old stubble remained in place as it had for years. Black slacks and polished shoes had replaced his jeans and boots. The white button-down, open at the neck, highlighted his tan skin and dark eyes. Her mouth watered. He looked more like a professional model than a firebrand Texas police detective.

Elle sank onto the plush couch. "Why are you still here and dressed like you're ready for a photoshoot?"

"Does my look impress you?"

"Answer my question."

"I'm the co-winner you're expecting. Randall Newman."

A heavyweight took up residence on her shoulders. "For real?"

"For real." Logan smiled the kind of smile you'd give a petulant child.

"Exactly how did you persuade Mr. Newman to give up the vacation of a lifetime?"

"Eric ran a background check on him. Newman isn't the smartest rooster in the barn. Seems he's been convicted of grand larceny and is out on parole. One call to clue in his probation officer that he'd booked a flight out of Texas without permission was all it took."

"So you took his place. Have the owners seen you?"

"Yup. Newman is tall, with dark hair and eyes. I look enough like his picture to pass." Logan carried the glass of wine to her. "You must have written one hell of a letter to win the contest. What if you'd lost?"

"Then my credit card would have suffered."

"Now that we know the owners are Ethridge's mark, I have to come clean with them."

The thought of being disqualified from the contest stoked her building anger. "If you and Eric mess up my chance to prove Ethridge is a crook, I'll never forgive either of you."

"Will you at least listen to what I have to say?"

Too upset to speak, she waved her hand.

"You've put a full-court press on the investigation into Ethridge Investments. Then all of a sudden, you drop everything to go on vacation. That was like waving a red flag in front of a bull. Eric knew you'd be pissed, so he asked me to come."

"Why'd you say yes?"

"That's not a question you should have to ask. We've been friends too long for me to say no."

"So, you're here to help me?" The word *friend* stabbed her in the heart.

"To keep you out of trouble."

Elle sipped at the wine. Eric had gone too far. "I'm not backing off just because you're babysitting me."

"After overhearing that Ethridge plans to scam the Fitzgeralds, I've changed my mind."

Elle let his statement sink in before she spoke. Her mind started churning. "Great. You can help me prove Brandon Ethridge is a criminal."

"There's one condition." Logan sat in the chair across from her. His muscular legs strained against his slacks. "I call the shots."

"For sure," she lied, keeping her gaze locked on his. "You're the expert." Every nerve cell in Elle's body was on high alert. Brain synapses continued to fire. Logan brought years of experience as a cop to the table.

His eyes narrowed to slits. "That was too easy. Ethridge is smart enough that the Feds haven't been able to gather enough to arrest him. If he has millions of dollars tucked away somewhere safe, you can bet your sweet ass he'll do whatever it takes to protect it. He's not going to turn the other cheek if he figures out what you're up to."

"I've done my homework. Nothing in his background suggests he's violent."

"He's a criminal. We don't know what he's capable of doing." He smiled when she held her hands up for a timeout. "Okay. It's my turn to listen."

His dark eyes peering over the rim of his wine glass was distracting. Elle breathed deeply, gathering her composure. She'd parlayed her degree in business into her own management search firm. Necessity had taught her how to deal with executives and people with inflated egos. She could handle this situation.

"I'm not stupid. My original goal was to gather evidence to present to the proper authorities. Now that we know why he's here at Castle Alainn, I'm open to a change in plans."

"Good to know." He lifted one eyebrow. She hadn't won him over yet.

"We still need his records. If you broke into his room and ran a memory dump of Ethridge's laptop onto a flash drive, it wouldn't be admissible. I don't have those restrictions." The nerves in Logan's jaw twitched, but he remained silent. Elle forged ahead. "I've spent weeks looking into Ethridge's background and learning his habits. Where he goes. What he eats. He loves lobster bisque, by the way. I'll bet you didn't know that he and that spoiled daughter of his live in a multimillion-dollar house." Logan had leaned forward. His steady gaze meant she had his attention and had surprised him with her detective work. "I learned a lot from his neighbors."

"You didn't." Logan's eyebrows pulled together. Again.

"You'd be amazed how willing people are to talk. Especially after I explained I was a reporter for *Business Tycoon Monthly*. I may have hinted that Ethridge was being considered for the Man of the Year Award."

Logan emptied his glass and placed it on an end table. "You are treading on thin ice."

"Like I said, I can do things that you and Eric can't."

"And you could find yourself in serious trouble. Did it occur to you that one of those neighbors might've mentioned your visit?"

A faint whiff of cologne drifted off Logan, assaulting her senses. She fought the urge to lean closer to him. He stared at her, waiting for a response.

"Let them. I used a fake name. Besides, there's no such magazine." To get his mind off her transgressions, she picked up his glass, walked to the small bar in the corner, and added a splash of wine. Elle walked behind his chair, leaned down, and returned his drink. "Drink up. The hotel mixer has started. Time to meet Ethridge and his daughter."

"Okay. But this conversation is far from over." Logan took one sip before he stood. His gaze dropped to her toes and slid back up.

"What?" She caught a glimpse of lust in his eyes. Then it was gone, replaced by total disinterest.

"You've grown up."

"Thanks." She lifted one eyebrow. "You're not much of a cop if you just noticed. That happened a long time ago."

Two

Logan held the door for Elle, drinking in the sight as she brushed past him into the hall. She moved with confidence. The slight sway of her hips was mesmerizing. Hell yes, he'd noticed she'd grown up. He'd watched her mature and blossom for years. By the time she'd entered high school, it had taken a Herculean effort not to drool when she entered a room.

He'd had good survival skills back then too. He'd heeded Eric's warning not to even think about messing with his sister. Elle glanced over her shoulder and caught him staring. She lifted one dark eyebrow but said nothing. This was going to be a rough week.

She stepped into the elevator and turned to face him. Elle breathed out a sigh. Her jaw tightened. The hardheaded girl he remembered from childhood looked up with a glare.

"It would be nice to have your help. If you're not willing, please don't interfere."

Logan dropped his hand to the small of her back as the elevator doors opened. His fingers heated from the warmth she generated. The soft spot he'd had for her hadn't diminished over the years. Spending time alone with her was going to be a true test for him. He wasn't in love with her, but he was sure as hell in lust.

He'd never felt so divided.

Eric was counting on his best friend to keep her safe. The only way he was going to pull that off was to keep his mind out of the bedroom and go along with her crazy plan. He could be risking his career, but if she got hurt, mentally or physically, he'd never forgive himself.

Even before they reached the lobby, the sound of music and people laughing filled the vast open space. Castle Alainn had been around for hundreds of years. A lot of the ancient opulence had been preserved. The lobby, with its marble floors and atrium, resembled an opera house he'd seen in a movie.

Red ribbons and bows dotted the walls and hung from the ceiling. A hand-carved, life-size nativity scene filled one corner. At the opposite end of the room, a huge Christmas tree with multicolored lights sat before a wall of windows. The curtains were open to show the blowing snow.

Elle's hand on his arm stopped him. "Ethridge is about ten feet in front of you."

"I got him. The blonde is his daughter?"

"Yes. Don't let Nicki's looks blind you. Her neighbors think she's unpolished." Elle chuckled. "Their words, not mine."

"You got the neighbors to swap gossip with you? I'm impressed."

"Don't laugh. I read that if you make people feel like you're a friend, they feel more comfortable speaking. Once I convinced them to let me inside, I'd take a quick look around their living room and pick a family picture or a piece of art to ask about. After we chatted for a minute, they usually relaxed and answered my questions."

"Interviewing 101."

Logan watched as Nicki Ethridge openly flirted with everyone from the male guests to the waitstaff. A tug on his sleeve pulled his attention to Elle. Her pupils flared.

"You're staring."

"Just checking the layout," he lied with a grin. Had he detected a bit of jealousy? "Let's get a drink and work the room."

Having Elle's hand tucked in the crook of his arm felt good as they travelled between the guests. They shook hands, chatted with a few couples, and then moved back into the mix.

Eventually, they found themselves a few feet away from Ethridge and his daughter, who were talking with a group of possible marks. He stopped and turned his back to the room. No way was Logan letting this opportunity pass. "We need to make nice with Brandon and Nicki. Think you can pull this off?"

"Of course."

Logan doubted Elle's acting ability. Hatred was a hard emotion to hide. He turned and casually moved to the Ethridges' circle and took charge of the introductions.

Elle's lips tightened when Logan used his real name. It had panicked her, but an idea on how to play Ethridge had just formed in Logan's mind.

Nicki quickly inserted herself next to him. She and Ethridge played off each other, reaffirming compliments and comments. Their behavior felt like a well-choreographed performance. The hair on the back of his neck vibrated.

Brandon, as they'd been instructed to call him, wore dark gray slacks and a red sweater. His salt-and-pepper hair gave him a distinguished appearance, but at the same time, he was almost pretty. Not one wrinkle marred his face, meaning he'd been born with great genes or he had an expert plastic surgeon. No way was he old enough to have a daughter in her late twenties.

Nicki's platinum-blonde hair, pale ivory skin, and bright red lips were all by design. A pale blue dress stopped at her ankles, showing off toenails polished to match her lipstick. The plunging neckline and high slit up the side of one leg left little to the imagination. Her style screamed sex and money.

"Aren't you just cotton candy for the eyes," Nicki purred. "When did you arrive?"

"A few hours ago. You?" Logan would use her flirting to his advantage.

"Dad and I flew into Denver yesterday. We waited in town until the blizzard eased before coming up the mountain. Noble Pass can be quite treacherous."

"I heard that at the airport. You're familiar with the area?"

Her smile answered before she spoke. "I can be. If you need a guide, I'm free."

Logan doubted if anything about her was *free*. "Thanks. I'll remember your offer."

He turned his body slightly so he could see Elle. Her expression was stone cold. Her gaze should have frosted Brandon's balls. Logan had to intervene. He leaned closer to Nicki.

"You'll have to excuse my friend. She doesn't warm up to strangers very well."

"So you're a couple?"

"Oh, hell no." He laughed.

"Well, I think she's jealous that you're talking to me. Don't you?"

"I'm not worried. Are you?"

"Not hardly." Nicki swept her long hair over one shoulder. "What line of business are you in?" She scanned his clothing. She probably knew how much each item cost. Good thing he'd splurged.

"I own a small chain of B and Bs. Nothing on the scale of the Castle Alainn, but they're profitable." The idea of making himself a potential target had come to him when he'd shaken hands with Brandon. The B and Bs belonged to his dad, but he would play along.

"How quaint." Her eyes sparkled with interest. "What are they called?"

"Texas Country Inns." Before she could quiz him further, he turned to Elle and extended his hand. "I see Liam and Alana have joined the party. We should say hello."

"Sure thing," Elle agreed, twining her fingers through his.

"Wait," Nicki said. "Why don't you two join us for an early-morning trip down the mountain?"

"I haven't skied in years, but I'm game." Logan flashed his pearly whites at Nicki.

"I'll have to pass," Elle said quickly. "I signed up for a refresher lesson in the morning."

"I'm sure that's a good idea." Nicki's attempt at an innocent smile failed. "We'll entertain Logan while you're busy."

"Works for me." Logan could feel Elle's gaze burning a hole in his cheek.

"We'll meet at the lift desk at nine." Nicki looped her hand into Brandon's elbow. Together they navigated through the crowd.

"I'll alert rescue to be ready in case you don't return." Elle smiled up at Logan, but her smoldering eyes held no humor.

"Nicki thinks you're jealous of my attention to her." He twirled a lock of Elle's dark chestnut hair around his finger. Thoughts of satin sheets slid through his mind.

"In your dreams." Her words were firm, but a smile played at the corners of her lips.

"Be glad Nicki misinterpreted your actions. Otherwise, Brandon and Nicki might have questioned your disdain."

"I'm sorry." Elle sighed. "Visions of my grandmother standing on her feet all day at the daycare center kept popping into my head. At her age, there's a big difference between volunteering a few hours a week and working full time."

Logan's heart melted a little. He'd never been able to stay mad at Elle. Hadn't he forgiven her when she'd crashed his new bicycle into the tree, worrying only about her scrapes and bruises? Then there was the time she'd sideswiped his car while turning into the driveway. Anyone else would've caught hell, but Elle had never been just anyone else to him.

"Interviewing people you'll never see again is one thing. Undercover work requires you to take on a role and stay in it for the duration. You have to be believable. We won't learn jack shit if we piss off Brandon and Nicki." Logan stopped, turning her to face him. "Can you do that?"

Elle's expression turned solemn. "Yes. I won't blow it."

"That's my girl." He caught her hand and restarted their trip across the room.

"You keep Nicki happy," Elle said. "I'll do the rest."

Logan didn't have time to respond. Liam and Alana Fitzgerald had left their group and were approaching. The couple not only owned the castle, but they were the sponsors of The Noble Pass Affaire Getaway.

Elle leaned close. "Look how the Fitzgeralds hold hands. Just the way they speak to each other tells me they are still deeply in love."

"You really are a romantic," Logan whispered. She was probably thinking of her parents. They'd died in a car wreck before he'd met Elle and Eric, but Logan had heard stories about their love for each other.

"Randall." Alana spoke first, leaning in for a handshake. "I see you met our other winner."

"Yes." Logan wouldn't have time to fill in the details, but he had to start somewhere. "I'd like to schedule a meeting with you tomorrow."

"Of course," Liam said. "Is there a problem?"

"Not yet, but I should have told you at check-in that my name isn't Randall Newman. It's Logan Ford."

Liam's shoulders stiffened. "Why did you use an alias?"

"It's important that you not reveal what I tell you. I'm a Texas police detective, and I need you to trust me. I apologize for not explaining right away." Logan had to gain their cooperation. "Tonight isn't the time to discuss this. Tomorrow, we can get behind closed doors, and I'll explain everything."

"I don't appreciate being deceived." A nerve in Liam's jaw twitched.

"Liam," Alana said. Her voice was soft and encouraging. "The least we can do is hear him out."

Liam's face relaxed as he looked down at his wife. Alana gave him a slight nod. He turned to Elle. "You're okay with this?" he asked.

"Yes. I promise that Logan and I will come to your office right after lunch tomorrow. We'll clear everything up then."

"Why not earlier?" Liam asked. "We've never had problems with our contest, and I'd like answers."

"This is my fault." Elle stepped forward. Her eyes were wide with panic.

"If you'll give me a chance, I know you'll understand. Elle and I made plans for the morning. Changing them will make certain people curious."

"We'll expect to see you two around one tomorrow," Alana said.

"Thank you," Logan said.

"Then it's settled." Alana took Liam's hand and practically dragged him away.

Liam didn't look happy, but he nodded slowly. "Your rooms are as expected?"

"They're beautiful," Elle said. "I appreciate the separate entrances and lock-off doors to the common room."

"Safety first," Liam said, cutting his gaze in Logan's direction. "We want our clientele to have a fun and safe visit."

"If we can do anything to make either of you more comfortable, please let us know." Alana guided Liam off to meet other guests.

Logan led Elle out of the crowd into one of the many alcoves. "You understand why I told Liam and Alana?"

"Yes. We have to prevent them from giving Brandon any money."

"After we explain things, they can help steer Brandon and his scheme toward me."

"You?"

"Yes. I hinted to Nicki that I was wealthy."

Elle grasped his arm. "You want her and Brandon to try and con you?"

"Brilliant. Right?"

"I wouldn't go that far." Elle squeezed, pulling his gaze to her fingers for a minute. "What if Brandon checks up on you?"

"I'll call my dad and alert him. If anyone calls for Logan Ford, they'll say he's on vacation in Colorado." With a quick scan of the room, he'd located Brandon and Nicki going into the restaurant with Liam and Alana.

"Let's get a bite to eat." He tilted his head toward the dining room. "We're going to be in surveillance mode. Think you can handle it?"

"Of course," Elle said. She ran her hands over her hips, smoothing out her dress. "Lead on."

Logan chuckled at Elle's enthusiasm. "I'll make a good cop out of you."

"I'm happy with my little management search firm. Nothing's better than working from home." She slipped her hand into the crook of his arm. "But I'm pretty good at reading lips."

Logan's chest swelled with pride. The warmth of her touch sent his brain floundering. *Now is not the time to be distracted.* She matched his long strides as they crossed the expanse of the hotel lobby to the restaurant.

"Welcome. Dinner for two?" the maître d'[1] asked.

Logan scanned the room, locating his targets. "The lady is a bit chilled. We'd like a table near the fireplace if possible."

---

1. http://eatocracy.cnn.com/2011/09/02/d-mystifying-the-maitre-d/

"Of course," he said. "One moment." He walked to the hostess and they chatted briefly. She smiled broadly and hurried to Elle and Logan.

"This way, please," she said, leading the two across the dimly lit restaurant.

Elle smiled and waved at the two couples while Logan held her chair. He seated himself with his back to Brandon. The hostess handed them menus and placed the wine list at his right elbow.

"Enjoy your meal," she said.

"Thank you," Logan responded, adjusting his position so Elle could see around him. "Smile. We're supposed to be having a nice dinner...just the two of us."

"Sorry. I'll do better," she said flashing her pearly whites. "I can't hear a word. Can you?"

Logan concentrated for a second, picking up a random word or two. The easy-listening music in the background wasn't loud, but it made eavesdropping difficult. "Not very well. We'll put your lip-reading skills to the test. Repeat anything you understand to me. Just try and make it look conversational."

The candle on the table flickered, sending shadows dancing across Elle's face. Logan couldn't take his gaze off her. It wasn't a chore for him to pretend he was interested in her. Regardless of Eric's many warnings and threats, Elle had always stirred deep feelings in him.

"Do you think she's really his daughter?" Elle leaned closer, no doubt pretending to flirt.

"No way. He's not old enough to have a child her age. I'll have Eric check that out for us."

"He'll do that?"

"He will after I tell him what we've learned. In the meantime, you can help by continuing to be impressed with my charm and immense wealth."

Elle's face lit up. Her eyes caught the glow from the flickering fire. "We're really going to send that bastard to prison."

"If we're lucky." The smile on her face stabbed him right in the heart.

"I'm very glad you're here." She extended her arm and reached for him.

Logan slid his hand under hers, wrapping his fingers around her delicate skin. He'd battled his feelings for her long enough. Either way, he was screwed.

Three

Logan's sudden silence troubled Elle. His strong fingers tightened around her hand. Suddenly, he pulled away, released her as if she'd bitten him.

"What is it?" she asked.

"Nothing." He glanced around the room, catching the sommelier's attention. "There's a particular wine I thought you'd like, but I can't remember the name."

"Really?" His rejection stung. He'd gone from being tender and romantic to ice cold. "When did you become a connoisseur?"

"Eric asked me to take care of you, not to involve you in an investigation." Logan pushed the wine list away, telling the sommelier to bring their best Cabernet Sauvignon.

"I'm a lot safer with you here."

Logan mumbled, "Depends on your definition of safe."

Their server arrived, ending their discussion. Logan ordered prime rib, rare. Elle chose the same only a smaller portion and cooked well done.

"A Texan ordering her beef well done. Your grandmother would be ashamed." The fun-loving, easygoing Logan had returned.

"That's true. She finally gave up trying to get me to eat raw meat."

He laughed. The sound wrapped around Elle like a strong pair of warm and inviting arms. "Rare is not raw."

"Close enough."

She shifted in her chair so it appeared she was looking at Logan. Truth be told, given the opportunity, Elle could easily lose herself in his dark eyes. For now, she turned her attention to Brandon at the next table.

It didn't take long to realize her lip-reading wasn't as good as she'd bragged. Keeping up with Brandon's words was almost impossible, but she snagged a few words.

A glass of wine appeared in front of her. She shifted her attention in time to see the sommelier walk away. "I missed the uncorking and tasting. How'd I do that?"

"You were staring at me." Logan chuckled. "At least, it looked that way. Did you learn anything?"

"That Brandon talks ninety miles an hour, and I'm not as good as I thought. I picked up a few words. Resort, riches, and worldwide. Oh, and investment."

"That's good. I heard him mention having a sense of urgency. That's the way these guys work. They convince the investor that the window to the deal is about to close, and if they don't want to lose out, they'll get on board quickly." The background music stopped briefly, and Logan stopped talking. "Liam just said they didn't have that much cash."

"Alana is very animated. Her hands are moving rapidly."

"She's against taking money from their retirement. Let's hope she sticks to her guns. Tomorrow we'll explain everything." The music restarted, ending Logan's chance to learn more. "After Brandon learns he can't clean out the Fitzgerald's bank account, maybe I can provide him with a new mark."

"It doesn't give you much time to build a background."

"Eric needs something to worry about other than his baby sister spending time with his best friend." Logan held up his glass in a toast.

Elle touched her glass to his. Surprised by his statement, she had to tease him. "So why would Eric worry about you and me up here in the mountains all alone? What could he possibly be afraid would happen?"

Logan's eyes narrowed to slits for a second. "Eric's an old mother hen when it comes to you."

Logan had evaded her question. She decided to let him get away with it, for now. "You don't think we're in danger?"

"Criminals can get violent if they're cornered. We just need to keep our intentions under the radar until we have enough evidence to turn over to the FBI."

"I presented them with enough complaints. They've done nothing."

"You don't know that. No agency, including the FBI, is going to tell you if they've launched an investigation."

Dinner arrived and both fell into silence as they ate. Even well done, her prime rib was tender and moist. Elle sliced off a piece and held out her fork. "Try this."

Logan's gaze met hers as he leaned across the table and slid the piece of meat off her fork into his mouth. Electricity, strong enough to incinerate the Christmas tree in the corner, charged back and forth between them.

"Not bad." He offered to share a bite of his prime rib, but she waved him off.

"They're right behind you." Elle and Logan pretended to ignore the two couples as they walked past, but she listened closely.

"It's important that you act now," said Brandon. "I have other investors waiting in line for this deal."

Logan placed his fork on his plate and leaned back. "Typical fraud talk. Try to convince the mark that they're going to miss out if they wait too long."

"We have to make sure the Fitzgeralds don't get ripped off." Elle had a lot of faith in Logan. His reputation as a crime solver was well known. "Fate sent you here to save them from disaster."

"Fate's name is Eric."

"So he's the only reason you came?" She was fishing, but she had to seize the moment.

Logan refilled her glass but not his own. "You know better."

"You're not drinking?"

"One of us has to keep a clear head." The corner of his mouth curved upward.

"Why, Mr. Ford," Elle said in her best heavy drawl. "Are you trying to get me drunk so you can take advantage of me?"

Again, Logan laughed. God she loved to hear the slow and sexy sound. She'd never get tired of it. "Don't make me give your pretty head a knuckle rub."

"You wouldn't dare." She joined his laughter.

"And I'd never take advantage of you."

Elle took a sip of wine. She'd barely kept herself from telling him that she wished he would. "I think I'm finished." She pushed the glass to the center of the table.

"Then let's get out of here." He motioned for the check, signed it, and then walked around behind her and held her chair as she stood.

"Thank you. You're such a gentleman."

His eyebrow lifted. "That's not the way you should think of me."

Before she could challenge his comment, he'd ushered her out into the lobby. His hand rested on her lower back. How would it feel against her bare skin? She pushed away those thoughts while studying his profile. Logan wasn't handsome in a pretty-boy way. His nose was slightly crooked, and a small scar bisected his eyebrow. Both had been the result of falling from a treehouse he and Eric had built. His walk, deliberate with a bit of a swagger, exuded a quiet but deadly confidence.

Once inside the common room of their suite, Logan called his dad and went into detail, outlining how he could help pull off the sting. Elle kicked off her heels and relaxed on the couch. Logan paced while he explained the situation. He glanced at her and smiled.

"I will. Tell Mom I love her too." Logan ended the call, walked to her, and kissed her on top of the head. "That's from Dad."

"You miss having them live closer?"

"Sometimes, but I understand their move to San Antonio was strategic. They do the biggest business in that area." His gaze returned to the phone. "I'll call Eric later."

"Want me to talk to him?"

"No." Logan's answer came quick and sharp.

"Why not?"

"By the time Eric finishes grilling you, you'll both be pissed. I'll keep him on point."

"His over protectiveness is getting old. Who I'm friends with, date, or have sex with is none of his damn business." She waved off the shocked look on Logan's face. "I understand that Eric felt he had to take over for our father, and I love him for it. He was too young to shoulder such a responsibility. Now it seems he's too old to let it go."

"He'll let go when the right man comes along. When he sees you're happy, he will be too."

Logan punched in a number and left a message for Eric to call. A knock on the door drew both of them to their feet.

"I'll get it." Logan leaned down and removed a small pistol from an ankle holster.

"You brought a gun?"

"Never without it. Hardest thing I've done in a while was checking my lockbox at the airport." His movement was fluid but strong as he checked to see who stood on the other side of the door. "Housekeeping."

The housekeeper offered to turn down their beds and build a fire. Logan thanked her, stating he'd handle the fireplace. True to his word, within minutes of closing the door, he had a roaring fire crackling, sending orange and red flames dancing.

Logan left the room and returned with his laptop. He'd kicked off his shoes, unbuttoned the top two buttons on his shirt, and rolled up his sleeves. The sheer casualness of the situation seeped into her soul, turning her muscles to putty.

His fingers moved across his keyboard. With his gaze locked on the computer screen, she watched as he shifted into cop mode.

"What are you working on?"

"Trying to brush up on our boy Brandon." Logan glanced up. "Damned slow Internet is killing me."

Elle didn't ask additional questions, allowing him to continue working. In the quiet, she planned tomorrow's activities. Logan, Nicki, and Brandon's ski outing would keep them busy for hours. Elle would use that time to again search for his laptop. She was taking a huge risk, but this was something she had to do. She snuggled deeper into the couch, watching Logan as he worked. Her eyelids grew heavy as images of hot, sweaty sex with him crept into her thoughts.

* * * *

Brandon's background check held no great surprises for Logan. He'd already guessed that Nicki was not Brandon's daughter. In fact, no record existed of him having fathered a child. Logan ran the name Nicki Ethridge through the system. He'd expected nothing, and that's exactly what he got...a handful of air.

Elle had fallen asleep. Her long dark hair had fallen across the pillow, circling back to softly caress her graceful neck. The vibration of his phone snapped him out of his daze. Eric was returning Logan's call.

"What's up?" he said, quickly moving into his bedroom so he wouldn't disturb Elle.

"You called me," Eric said. "Something wrong with Elle?"

"No, but there's been a change of plans, and I need your help."

"I'm listening." The hesitant tone in Eric's voice came through loud and clear.

Logan quickly explained that the owners were the target of Ethridge's next fraud. "I'm going to alert the Fitzgeralds. Make sure they pass on the deal."

"So how can I help?"

"I've started laying the groundwork to make myself a replacement target. I've spoken with my dad, and he's on board. A benefit of being a junior. He'll alert his people to cover for me. I need you to make sure a background check on me looks good."

"Shit." Eric ground out the words. "I should've known she'd sucker you into some wild-ass scheme."

"This is my plan. My idea. Her being here will actually help me pull this off."

"Keep her out of it. Your mission is to keep her out of trouble."

Logan walked to the door into the common room where she lay sleeping on the couch. A hard tug on his heart surprised him. Could a relationship with Elle work? Would Eric come around? "Nothing is going to happen to her. I'll make sure of that."

"If Ethridge discovers you're running a game on his game, he might lash out. The Weather Channel said that Noble Pass is closed. What if she gets hurt or you need help?"

"Will you stop? I've got this."

"Fine. I'm counting on you."

Logan ended the call. He walked straight through to Elle's side of the suite. He turned back her covers, flipped on the light in the bathroom, and then returned to the common room. For a few seconds, he stood over her and watched her sleep. He studied her features, noting she appeared much more angelic this way than awake and arguing with him.

He slid his arms under her and lifted her in one smooth motion. Elle's eyes fluttered open but then closed as she nestled her head against his shoulder. Damn, he couldn't resist the urge to stand still and hold her for a minute, but the longer she stayed in his arms, the harder putting her down would be. He carried her to her bed and gently laid her on the sheet.

Elle turned onto her side. A slight smile played at the corners of her lips, but she didn't open her eyes. He leaned down and softly kissed her cheek before pulling the blanket over her body. He turned off the light and left the room, closing the door behind him.

It was going to be a long night.

Four

Elle woke to the aroma of coffee. She pushed back the covers and discovered her new black dress bunched around her waist. Logan had put her to bed. She hoped that she'd been properly covered at the time. Hearing that she exposed the lace thong she'd worn last night would be embarrassing. She put her feet on the floor and straightened her clothes.

A memory flashed through her mind. She touched a spot on her cheek. Had she dreamed that Logan had kissed her?

"Rise and shine." Logan's playfulness gave her a morning smile. "I'm coming in on the count of three, so cover up," he called out.

"I'm up," she answered. "And ready for that coffee that I hope you're bringing me."

He strolled in carrying two cups as if this were something he did every day. Gray warm-ups hung loosely at his hips; his bare chest sported a sprinkling of dark hair. Elle's gaze tracked that trail until it disappeared under his waistband.

"Good morning." He held a cup close enough for the aroma to wake up her taste buds.

"Sorry. It's been a few years since I've seen you half-naked." She grabbed the coffee and took a big sip. The hot liquid seared off a layer of tongue as she swallowed, probably matching the color of the burn rushing up her cheeks.

Logan walked to the only chair in the room and sat. "Yeah. I was probably seventeen the last time you and Eric went water-skiing with me." Logan's gaze travelled across her body. "Your dress looks worse than you do. That last glass of wine put you out like a light."

"I never drink four glasses." Elle peered into the mirror. "My eyes look awful."

"You look great. Besides, you were nervous." He pushed himself to his feet.

"No. I was careless and stupid." Elle glanced at the clock. "You'd better get going. Nicki will worry if you're late."

Logan moved across the room like a very fast cat. He stood toe-to-toe with her, hooked his index finger under her chin, and gently lifted until their gazes locked. "I'm not worried about her opinion of me."

Heat bloomed in her belly and headed south. "Exactly whose opinion do you care about?"

His mouth opened but didn't speak. She mentally pleaded with him to say something. He leaned down and brushed her forehead with his lips. Frustration cooled the pool of heat forming between her thighs.

"Have a good day." Elle had to get him out of her bedroom before she kissed him or punched him, whichever came first. Besides, he had a ski date, and she had a plan to execute.

"Damn it, Elle. You're as transparent as cellophane. Do not break into Brandon's suite again."

Elle kept her composure and bit back a sharp retort. "Yes, dear."

"Okay. I sounded a bit bossy. I just don't want you to get into trouble."

"You mean Eric doesn't want me to get into trouble."

Logan's expression turned icy. "If that's what you want to believe."

There for a fleeting heartbeat, she'd hoped he'd say that he was worried about her. When that didn't happen, Elle motioned him out of the room. "You'll have to excuse me. I have to get ready for my ski lesson. I hear the instructor is an Olympic medal winner and is extremely hot."

She grabbed her brand new Patagonia sweater and pants out of the drawer. She removed her waterproof Eddie Bauer boots from the closet and placed them next to her bed. She ignored Logan as she brushed past him on the way to the dresser, where she selected a lacy red bra and matching panties.

"Oh, lord," Logan groaned. He left her bedroom, closing the door behind him.

Elle chuckled on her way to the bathroom. She showered but didn't dress. Instead, she took her time moisturizing her arms and legs. After a long twenty minutes, she opened the door and called Logan's name. Confident he'd left; she opened her closet, removed the blonde wig from its box, and slipped it on her head. She selected a long-sleeve beige sweater, and matching slacks. A colorful scarf around her neck matched her red flats. Her plan had worked the first time she had gotten into Brandon's suite. Could she pull off pretending to be Nicki again?

She took the elevator down to the sixth floor, walked to Ethridge's suite, and removed the Do Not Disturb sign from the door handle. The housekeeping cart was parked four doors away, making her timing perfect. Doing her best to slow her racing heart, she stood still, one hand hovering over the handle, the other holding the sign in the air. She waited what seemed like an eternity, but finally the housekeeper stepped into the hall. Elle went into action.

"Oh, no," she said loudly, and in her best panicked voice. She hurried to one of the women waving the Do Not Disturb sign. "Before I hang this on the door, will you put fresh towels in the bathroom?" Elle didn't wait for a response. She spun on her heel, marched back to the room, and pretended to panic. "My purse. I left it inside."

For a moment, she thought the woman wasn't going to comply with her request. Elle decided to be more assertive. She stabbed one hand on her hip and waved the sign. "My husband will be up to rest soon, and I don't want him disturbed."

That did the trick, as the housekeeper filled her arms with towels and washcloths and hurried toward the room. Elle laid a five-dollar bill on the top towel, turned, and started toward the elevator. Before the doors slid open, she heard the woman enter the suite. Elle spun on her heels, rushed back, and entered the room.

"Better get my purse," Elle explained, taking the towels from the housekeeper. "I'll put these away."

The woman slid the five in her uniform pocket and nodded.

"Thank you." Elle held her breath until the door snapped closed. She quickly opened it and replaced the Do Not Disturb sign.

Her charade had eaten up a total of forty-three minutes, leaving her with plenty of time to finish the search she hadn't completed yesterday. She slid back the closet doors, and there, sitting inside an open suitcase, was a laptop. Her heart pounded as she knelt down. Carefully, she lifted the top and turned on the computer. Her fingers trembled as she opened the control panel, inserted a flash drive, and then clicked the command to back up the files. As soon as the process was finished, Elle logged off and pocketed her evidence.

She stopped at the door. What was she forgetting? The towels. After all, Brandon or Nicki had placed the Do Not Disturb sign on the door. Elle rolled them into a bundle, tucked them under her arm, and quickly returned to her suite.

Once she'd closed the door behind her, Elle let out the breath she'd been holding, in a whoosh. Her knees seemed to have lost all muscle strength. Elle sank down in the easy chair next to the window and stared out at the snow-covered landscape.

A giggle rolled up her chest and bubbled out. She'd done it. Pulled it off. She'd brazened her way into the suite and gotten what she'd come to Colorado after. She removed the wig, kicked off her shoes, and then rested her feet on the ottoman. She took the flash drive from her pocket and held it in her hand. For a few minutes, she enjoyed a job well done.

Elle had planned to wait for Logan so they could study the contents of the flash drive together. And maybe she'd gloat a little. Time passed too slowly. Soon, she was pacing, checking the clock every few minutes. She'd failed to ask how long the ski outing would last. It was almost noon, and she couldn't wait any longer. She got up, retrieved her laptop, and pushed the on button. Tingles of expectation and anxiety set off all her nerve endings. She inserted and opened the drive.

* * * *

Brandon almost lost his concentration. Almost lost his skis. Almost lost his self-control right there heading downhill. The unique series of vibrations coming from his cell had announced that someone had accessed his computer. The alarm would buzz every three minutes until he recognized the message. His only recourse was to keep calm.

He'd paid dearly for the safeguard. A hacker might gain entrance to his computer, but they couldn't open his private files. The fail-safe encrypted the files, protecting them from theft.

The IT company that had sold him the program was already in the process of identifying the bastard. Once he got to the bottom of this fucking mountain, he'd call, and they'd identify who'd tampered with his laptop.

Nicki was just ahead of him. She and Logan appeared to be relaxed and enjoying each other. She could keep him entertained while Brandon took care of business. Goddamn, she was going to flip out.

* * * *

Logan had sensed a change in Brandon's demeanor the minute they'd returned from skiing. He'd rushed through turning in his equipment. Then he'd hurried to the far corner and dug his cell out of his pocket. He'd rejoined Logan and Nicki and announced he had an important call to make. He'd left Nicki with Logan.

Logan removed his outerwear, rolled it up, and stored it in his backpack. He and Nicki walked inside the resort. She moved close to him, almost leaning into him.

"I could use a hot chocolate to warm my bones. How about you?"

Logan welcomed a little one-on-one time with Nicki. "You're on. Brandon took off in a hurry. Should we wait for him?"

"No. Besides, I need a few minutes without him around."

Logan steered her to a table close to the front. "Daddy Dearest getting on your nerves?"

Nicki's laugh was a well-rehearsed sound that even the untrained ear would recognize as phony. "Something like that."

After they'd ordered, Logan took the opportunity to try to get her to relax. "Thanks for inviting me today. I'd forgotten how much I enjoy skiing."

"You got your feet under you pretty fast. No doubt you've always been athletic."

It was Logan's turn to chuckle. "More likely muscle memory kicked in, saving me from winding up flat on my back or wrapped around a tree. Obviously, you and your dad hit the slopes a lot."

Nicki launched into a story about the many different ski vacations she'd enjoyed. He tried a couple of times to get her to talk about Brandon, but she'd steer the conversation back to all the places a person could vacation if they had enough money.

"Who runs your business when you're away?" Nicki leaned forward.

"My father. He has a good head for business. After I opened the fourth B and B, I hired him as my chief operations officer. He's good at keeping the books. I just wish he had more savvy when it comes to investing my money." Logan stood, ending the conversation. He intended to leave Nicki wanting more. "I enjoyed the day, but I'd better get back. Like your dad, I have some calls to make."

Logan signed the tab and left the coffee shop. It took great restraint not to rush to the elevator. The closer he got to the room, the harder his heart pounded. Shit, he was acting like a kid. He'd only been gone a few hours, yet he'd missed Elle.

He jammed the card key into the slot, opened the door, and called out. "Decent or not, I'm coming in."

"I've been waiting for you," Elle said. "Come see what I have."

Her excited tone spoke volumes. She'd broken into the Ethridge's' suite after he'd asked her not to. Logan dropped his backpack on the couch and walked to her bedroom doorway. "Damn it, Elle. If you—" A swath of blonde hair spread across the foot of her bed caught his attention. "The wig again? Do I want to know what you've done?"

"Not if you're going to judge me. I came to Castle Alainn to get proof. It's the only reason I'm here." She gave Logan a go-to-hell look and stood. Carrying the laptop, she walked past him to the bar in the common room.

"You're damn proud of breaking the law."

"My battery is low. Hang on while I get the cord."

He caught her by the arm as she passed. She turned into him. Her breasts brushed against his chest, stalling his brain for a second. "Damn it, Elle." Frustration bubbled up. "You could've been seen."

"I opened a list of client names, but there are other larger files that I haven't opened yet. There's a lock next to them. With or without your help, I'm going to get them open."

"Elle." He wanted to be pissed, but honestly, hadn't he known what she'd planned to do today? He was as guilty as she was.

"You understand. Don't you?" Her eyes were full of hope.

"Yes." Logan, lost in her nearness, lowered his head fully intending to taste her lush mouth. She rose on her toes to meet him. A second before contact, his brain started working, and he stepped back. "Get your cord."

He turned away and quickly rearranged himself. What would she think if she noticed his erection? Two hands slid up his chest to his shoulders. She leaned into him.

"You almost kissed me." Her warm breath caressed his neck.

"But I didn't."

"Why did you stop?"

"You know why." His resolve was slipping. Her breasts pressed into his back, sending streaks of fire south. "Kissing you would change everything. The dynamics of our relationship would never be the same." Erection be damned, he had to make her understand. He took a bolstering breath and turned to face her.

Eyes dark as night stared up at him. The gold specks he'd always admired seemed to sparkle even brighter than usual. Lush, pouty lips parted slightly, begging to be devoured.

He did the only thing he could. He buried both hands in her hair and kissed her.

Her lips parted as she pressed against him, moaning softly. An explosion came from somewhere deep inside, and he swept his tongue inside her mouth, probing and tasting the sweetness that was uniquely Elle. This was no soft and easy exploration to see if a flame existed and might grow. This was a full-on assault between two starving people who could only be satisfied by intimate contact with each other. A battle that had been brewing for years.

Her hands roamed up and down his back, stopping at his waist. Cool air hit his skin as his shirt slid from his pants. Logan's breath caught as her warm fingers massaged his tight muscles. He looped one hand around her waist and tugged her snug against his body. His erection pushed against her soft flesh, but she only dug her fingers in deeper as their tongues fought for supremacy.

Insanity had taken hold of them both. Somebody had to slam on the brakes. Could he stop? This would be the hardest task he'd ever faced. Logan tore his lips from hers.

"Elle, baby. We can't." He lowered his forehead to lean against hers. Both of them struggled to catch their breath.

"Sure we can." She'd spoken so softly he'd had to strain to hear her words. She took a couple of steps backward. Looking up at him, she hit him with a piercing look. "Maybe you meant to say that we shouldn't?" Her gaze dropped to the most painful erection he'd ever had. "Saying we can't? That's crap."

Shit. He'd really screwed things up. "You're making jokes?"

"There's nothing funny about that kiss. Or your reaction to it." Her breathing was irregular, and her pupils had dilated.

"Elle." God, he was truly a bastard. If she took a single step forward, he would pull her into his arms and kiss her until she begged for release. "You're a beautiful woman. I'd have to be dead not to want you. But you're excited because of your recent acquisition." He nodded toward the flash drive. "Adrenaline is pumping through your veins, like water through a fire hose. After you crash, I don't want you to regret how you celebrated."

The air between them chilled as they stared at each other. No way could he tell her that he'd fallen for her years ago. Up here in the mountains, snowed in and on an adventure, she was too vulnerable.

"One of these days, you'll figure out that I'm capable of making my own choices and decisions."

Her independence and strength just made him want her more. "I don't want you avoiding me after we get back to Texas because you regret one of those decisions."

A shrill ring ended their discussion. Logan turned to the bar and picked up the room phone. "Hello."

"Mr. Ford, Alana Fitzgerald here. I've ordered coffee and a plate of our special recipe homemade muffins for our meeting. Is there anything special you'd like to add?"

She'd caught Logan off guard, and he paused to get his brain back on track. "Sounds like you've thought of everything." He glanced at his watch. "We'll see you in a few minutes."

"Yes. Fair warning, Liam is still a bit miffed and needs convincing."

"I can do that. He might feel better if he calls the Fort Worth Police Department and asks for Eric Reagan." Logan ended the call and repeated the conversation to Elle. "Give me a few minutes to shower and change. We have to persuade Liam to let this play out."

"And wasn't that call perfect timing? I'll change and be right out." Elle leaned around him and picked up her laptop. She tucked it under her arm and walked to her room.

Logan considered going after her, but didn't trust himself near a bed and her at the same time. As bad as he needed a long cold shower, he settled for a quick in and out. Until the day before leaving for Castle Alainn, he'd owned very few dress clothes. His wardrobe had consisted of casual stuff and various styles of boots and a couple pairs of tennis shoes.

He slid on his black, hundred-percent virgin wool slacks that had set him back a pretty penny, a blue Italian cotton shirt, and then slipped his feet into calf leather loafers. Damn, how anyone got used to dressing this way was a mystery. Give him a pullover, a pair of jeans, and western boots any day.

Elle was waiting in the common room. "Wow. You look like a million bucks."

"I'll take that as a compliment." Logan tugged at his shirt collar. "As usual, you look great. Of course, I'm a little prejudiced."

She wore brown boots, a long tan skirt, and a brown sweater. A low ponytail held all those dark waves off her face, highlighting her cheekbones and creamy complexion.

"Thanks."

Her tone, low and flat, cut through him. A snake slithering though the grass couldn't have felt any lower than Logan did at that moment. No way could he leave the room with her feelings hurt.

Logan walked to her and cupped her cheek in his hand. "When the time is right, you're going to make a decision about us. Left to me, you'll be whispering my name before dark." He kissed her softly, rimming her lips with his tongue before stepping back. She smiled at him, lifting a huge weight off his shoulders. The front of his pants got tight again.

"I like being the decision maker." She ran her fingers across his chin.

"You're going to be the death of me," Logan said, behind a laugh.

Five

"I wish we didn't have to go." Elle's heart pounded against her rib cage. Logan's kiss had sent desire gnawing at her very foundation. All these years, he'd ignored her, treated her like a little sister. Had he thought she didn't care for him, or had Eric interfered?

"Me too." Logan opened the door for her, paused, and looked up and down the hall.

"What are you looking for?" Elle struggled to get her brain back on track. Logan appeared to have returned to normalcy.

"I'm wondering if you made your film debut when you broke into the Ethridge suite."

"I checked before the first time. There aren't any cameras in the halls or elevators."

"Good. You being arrested for breaking and entering would be a surefire way to end this project." Logan walked the length of the hall, returned, and then pushed the elevator button.

"I'd tell them you weren't involved. You'd just have to work without me."

"Like that's going to happen." He tugged her ponytail. "You okay?"

"Me?" Elle decided she had nothing to lose by telling the truth. "Of course not. I keep remembering how I felt when we kissed."

"It was worth remembering." Logan wrapped his arm around her shoulder. "I don't know about you, but nothing gets my mind off wanting to have hot, sweaty sex, like strong coffee and warm muffins."

"So you're not pissed at me for breaking the law?"

"I'm still working on that." His mischievous smile said he was joking.

"Try to see it from my point of view. When my parents died, Nan opened her arms and house to Eric and me. She never once complained. She worked hard, provided us with everything we needed, and taught us to put a little money into a nest egg. Her savings was her way of ensuring she had a simple but decent retirement."

"I love her too. With Mom and Dad always working, your grandmother gave me the guidance I wasn't getting at home. I feel your sense of loyalty, but there's a right way to bring Ethridge to justice. Nothing we learn from the information you stole is admissible."

"So you've said. But if it points us in the right direction—" The elevator doors opened, and Nicki Ethridge stepped inside.

"Logan." She stopped halfway inside. The smile she'd given him vanished when she saw Elle. Nicki took a card from her purse and handed it to him. "When you have a minute, give me a call." She stepped back and let the doors close.

"Wow. That was awkward." Elle laughed, but jealousy rested right under the surface. "My skin should be burning from the blistering look she gave me."

The elevator stopped, and the doors swished open, ending their conversation. Right before they entered the Fitzgeralds' office, Logan caught her arm.

"You're sure no one saw you?"

"The maid who let me in. If by chance someone does question her, she'll remember that a blonde woman asked for help."

"Damn it, Elle."

The conversation ended when Alana opened the door. "Come in. The muffins are still warm."

It took less than an hour for Logan and Elle to share all the information they had on Brandon Ethridge and his investment scheme. Elle told her grandmother's story. She tried to show that he had no conscience.

She had never seen Logan in a professional capacity. Her heart expanded with pride as he presented his plan to Liam and Alana. He was not only precise, he was personable.

"Ethridge is smart. He has good lawyers who protect him, and he's proven he can outsmart the authorities. We intend to stop him from destroying anyone else's retirement."

Liam had been full of questions. He'd listened intently but had remained noncommittal the entire time. His gaze scanned the documents Logan had laid out on the conference room table.

Alana reached across the table and rested her hand on top of her husband's. "All they're asking for is our silence. It's the least we can do."

He looked up at Elle. "How's your grandmother?"

"She's gone back to work. Moved into a smaller house." Elle's eyed filled with tears. "My brother and I are all the family she has left. Nan is a proud woman. She refuses to accept financial help from us."

Liam smiled, patting Elle on the shoulder. "Your grandmother is fortunate to have you. We lost our grandson in a skiing accident last year. We've been considering selling the resort or turning it over to a management team."

"Brandon Ethridge will try to use your grief to his advantage," Logan said.

"It won't work," Liam said. "Not after hearing the truth about him."

Elle and Logan said their good-byes, but she stopped at the door and returned to Liam. "This place wouldn't be the same without you and Alana. Your charm and love for each other makes the castle warm and welcoming. I'll bet your grandson loved being here and wouldn't want you to sell."

Elle hugged Liam and Alana, then hurried out. Logan paused. His dark eyes sparkled.

"What?" Elle asked. Her heart expanded. Breath caught. His expression confused her. Was it pride, confusion, or affection radiating from his face?

"You're amazing." He cupped her cheeks and kissed her.

Elle melted into him. Right there in the lobby without thought as to who might be watching, she slipped her arms around his waist and returned his kiss.

"Thank you." She barely managed to force out the words. She'd really wanted to beg for more.

"My pleasure." He turned her toward the restaurant. "I don't know about you but I'm starving. I didn't eat a muffin."

A few minutes later, they had been seated, and bowls of steaming hot chili were sitting in front of them. According to the menu, this meal was guaranteed to defrost the body and warm the soul.

Elle wasn't sure she could handle much more heat. Every cell in her body had fired, and only one thing was going to cool her off. Logan.

She reminded herself why she'd come to Castle Alainn.

Elle checked the nearby tables before she spoke. Privacy was critical. Luckily, everyone must have eaten earlier. Having a late lunch worked well to ensure they wouldn't be overheard. "Surely you know someone who can unlock Brandon's files. Someone not associated with law enforcement."

Logan finished his bite, washed it down with a sip of beer, and studied his spoon for a long minute. "I'll see what I can do when we get back to the suite."

Her request had put Logan in a difficult position. His willingness to support her, to help her right this wrong, touched her heart. For him to agree so easily, spoke volumes. He was doing this for her. Deep down she'd known it for years. Had she and Logan been in love all this time and ignored or refused to admit it? Had fate given her the chance to answer that question?

"Thank you." She slid her hand across the table palm up. He wrapped his fingers through hers and squeezed.

"Let's get to it." Logan asked for the bill, signed it, and then stood.

She took his hand and walked to the elevator. The doors had closed when Elle remembered Nicki's request. "What do you think Nicki wanted?" Elle laughed when his right eyebrow lifted. "Besides your body."

"My money. I suggested that I might be disappointed in my current investment strategy."

"Smart. You should call when we get to the room."

"No. Let her wait. After Liam and Alana turn them away, I'm willing to bet that I'll become a serious target."

"If they come after you, anything you learn can be used against them. Right?"

"Right." Logan slid his card key into the door lock.

"Then I hope that works, even if it requires exposing you to that female piranha."

Logan glanced over his shoulder. "I'm touched that you'd worry about me."

"You misunderstand. I worry that you'll fall under her spell and slip up," she said, walking past him into the suite.

His laugh followed her. She loved the quick and hearty sound. It made her knees weak as hell.

"Okay, smart girl. Get out your laptop." He pulled his cell from his pocket. How could he switch from oozing sex to serious detective mode in the blink of an eye?

Elle set her laptop on the bar, turned it on, and waited for it to boot up. Logan was still on the phone when the program loaded. He winked at her. That simple gesture sent her heart dancing in her chest.

"What's your email address?"

She answered him and then retrieved a coffee pod, dropping it in the dispenser and pressing the on button. Not that she needed the caffeine. Her nerves were already spring boarding around her body like a kid on a trampoline.

"Fix me a cup too, please."

"What do we do next?" She selected another pod and waited for the first cup to finish.

"My friend is sending a program for me to install on your laptop. It's top of the line and should open your stolen files."

Strong hands slid around her waist, pulling her close. Logan's face pressed into her neck. "You smell good enough to eat."

Laughter bubbled out of her. She couldn't deny it sounded like a corny line, but it was also a great idea. She turned into his arms and kissed him. His tongue penetrated her mouth, and the ridge of his erection pressed against her belly. She leaned into him, wanting to feel his need. She deepened the kiss, putting herself out there, leaving no question as to what she wanted. Logan's arms drew her in tighter. Elle cupped his cheek, rubbing her palm against the stubble. How would it feel against her skin?

Logan moaned a low rumble. His chest vibrated, generating electric shocks that travelled through her system. Why had she waited so long to show him her feelings? The wait was over.

"Elle. This is your call." His voice was soft against her lips. His head tilted back, and his gaze zeroed in on her face. He studied her as if looking for a sign.

His words wrapped around her and filled her heart. Desire shifted to need. Her kiss was her answer. He tunneled his hands in her hair. Elle's fingers worked furiously to liberate the buttons on his shirt. She tugged until his chest was bare. God, he was beautiful. For a second, she rested her face on him, letting the heat from his skin blend with hers. The feathery kisses she placed across his chest and neck weakened her knees. This was really happening.

"My turn." He pulled her sweater over her head and made quick work of her bra, adding them to the growing pile of clothes on the floor. His gaze raked across her breasts. "You're more beautiful than I imagined. I could look at you forever."

Elle swept her hands over his hard, lean muscles, flexing her fingers against the shapes and contours of his body. Silk over rock. Logan dropped kisses on her cheeks and neck. She prayed he'd never stop, but he stepped back and removed the rest of her clothes.

"Perfection," he said as his eyes raked across her body.

Unsure she could speak intelligently, she whispered, "Bed."

"I thought you'd never ask." Logan swept her into his arms, carried her into her room, and carefully put her down. Before removing his pants, he pulled a condom from his wallet and placed it on the nightstand. Then he rid himself of the rest of his clothes.

Elle took full advantage of those few moments. His naked body was a work of art. The muscles in his back rippled with his every movement. She'd had a few lovers, but none of them had sported an erection the size of Logan's. He cleared his throat. Caught staring, she could only laugh.

"You're quite impressive." Her words came out over a dry and raspy throat.

"I aim to please." A chuckle, the one that always weakened her knees, rolled up and out of him. "You're pretty damn awesome yourself."

He sat next to her. His hands followed his eyes as he stroked her body, searing the sensation of his touch inside her heart. He seemed to be memorizing every detail as he travelled. Slowly, he lowered his head, gently caressing her lips with his. He filled his hands with her swollen breasts, rolling and pinching her nipples into tight peaks. When he leaned over and pulled a tip into his mouth, the ache low in her belly intensified. Elle's back bowed, instinctively rising to offer him more.

She murmured his name as his hand traversed her body. A rush of desire ricocheted through her nervous system. She'd imagined this moment. Painted erotic pictures in her mind of the two of them locked in an embrace. Nothing could have prepared her for this moment of passion.

Logan's fingers and mouth blistered and soothed until she was writhing with need. Her hands had travelled their own path, stroking his bare skin. His muscles quivered under her fingers. She boldly caressed and explored every inch of his body.

Logan moved on top of her, parting her thighs with his knee. He kissed her breasts, running his tongue along the underside. Elle was ready to beg for more. His hand slid down her body. The palm of his hand caressed her stomach. His fingers were streaks of fire slowly sliding downward. Every nerve ending in her body came alive. The ache between her thighs turned to agony.

At last, he touched her. Elle cried out when he spread her and inserted a finger. She opened for him, baring herself and needing flesh against flesh. Her blood raced through her veins and pounded in her ears.

"More," she whispered.

Logan moaned a deep, mouth-watering sound and continued his slide down her body until he reached her core. He parted her and leaned in for a kiss. The universe disappeared. She lifted her hips, silently encouraging him to keep going.

His hand slid under her hips, lifting her to just the right angle. His tongue took over, and all reason abandoned her. Her body quivered. Her hands raced over his shoulders, lingered as his muscles trembled. She couldn't take any more. "Logan," she moaned. "Please."

"Hmm," he hummed against her flesh.

She lost it. Her entire body vibrated with life. She shattered, grasping his head and holding him to her until the convulsions subsided. Exhausted, she pulled him to her.

He rested his head on her belly, allowing her to return to this world. When her heart rate slowed, he lifted his head and kissed her breasts, moving from one to the other. Slowly and with incredible patience, he rekindled her need for him.

Elle groaned as he pulled away and reached across her for the condom. She watched his every movement as he deftly slid it over his massive erection.

"Come here." She pulled him over her; she spread her legs wider, giving him free entry. Her heart squeezed when she saw more than passion in Logan's dark eyes. He cared for her, just as she did for him. Years of secretly wanting each other ended right now. "Logan," she whispered.

He pushed inside her, moving slowly, inching his way into her body, pausing to allow her to adjust. His entrance alone had almost sent her over the edge. She drew her legs up high, wrapped them around his hips, and dug her fingers into his butt. She pulled him until he relinquished control and slammed home.

They found their rhythm quickly. The faster and harder he thrust, the closer she came to exploding. He slid his hand down her body until his fingers found her center. She tried to speak.

Wanted to express her feelings for him but found herself lost in the sensation.

"Elle." His face was taut with restraint. Sweat had beaded across his forehead, but he continued driving her closer and closer to the edge.

His eyes fixed on hers, demanding she give her all. Demanding she surrender. Demanding she release herself into his hands. Nothing existed except right here, right now. Her climax exploded. Her body convulsed. Stars shattered in front of her eyes, and ecstasy filled her soul.

He thrust himself deep inside her. His body stilled, spine straightened. A primal growl roared from him as he shuddered and pulsed. Logan's release gave her an instant peace she'd never known before. She cradled him in her arms until his breathing returned to normal. Spent and sweating, they lay in silence.

"I'm squashing you." He lifted his weight off her.

"No. Stay here." She pulled him to her, relishing his body pressing her into the mattress.

His lips covered hers in a gentle caress. She melted into him. "You look sexy as hell. You wear your orgasms well."

"Thank you." A dull ache in her heart replaced the euphoria when he rolled away from her. Now that their lovemaking was over, how would they go forward? She couldn't do friends with benefits. The bonds of friendship had been shattered all to hell. She'd never regret making love with him, and for now, she'd live in the moment. If this had been nothing more than sex for fun, it would break her heart.

Logan went into the bathroom, and then returned to her bed. He kissed her long and hard. Then he lay down beside her and pulled her head onto his chest. They remained in that embrace for a long time. Awake, silent, holding each other close.

He ran his fingers through her hair. "I hate to say this, but we—"

"Don't say we shouldn't have done this. Just don't."

"Shouldn't have?" Logan rolled off the bed, stood, and pulled on his underwear. "You must think I'm a sorry bastard. I don't regret one second of it, and I don't think you do either." He picked up her panties and dropped them on her bare belly. "I was going to say, we need to check your email. Let's download the program and get some work done."

Elle sat up and reached for him, but he'd already picked up his pants and left her room, closing the door behind him. She'd jumped to conclusions and ruined something beautiful. She slipped on her panties and slacks and hurried to the common room for the rest of her clothes.

The sound of the water running from Logan's shower tempted her. What if she stripped and joined him? Could she convince him she was sorry for assuming the worst? Should she tell him that she'd had a crush on him since the day she first laid eyes on him? Probably not.

Elle picked her clothes up off the floor and returned to her room. She hung up her things, tossed a pair of jeans and an old sweatshirt onto the bed along with clean underwear. The Internet was so slow that downloading the program was going to take a while, which meant she had time for a bath. Elle filled the jetted tub with warm water, dumped in the entire guest bottle of bubbles, and stripped. After stepping into the tub, she sat and pushed the button activating the jets. Within seconds, bubbles came up to her chin. Elle leaned back, closed her eyes, and remembered. Logan had woken a passion in her that had been growing for years. Her body had come alive with a vibrancy she'd never experienced.

If this, whatever this was between them, ended badly, the pain would last a lifetime.

Six

Logan didn't know Elle's password, so checking to see if the ghostwriter program had been received wasn't an option. Had she gone to sleep while he'd been in the shower? He eased open her door. A soft hum from the bathroom drew his attention.

Elle was singing. His fingers wrapped around the knob. She might be upset if he just walked in on her. He chose the smarter route and knocked.

"You need to check your email." The sound of water splashing sent blood rushing south. Elle in a bathtub with him sounded like pure delight.

"Be right there." The door opened, and Elle stood there smiling, wearing an oversized white robe. The coat of arms for Castle Alainn had been embroidered just above her left breast.

"Sorry. I didn't intend to stay in the tub so long."

Logan breathed in her scent. Definitely some type of flower. He had no idea what kind, but he'd know before they left the resort. After they got home, he'd have a bouquet of them delivered to her on a regular basis. "Maybe next time we should bathe together."

Elle lifted on her tiptoes and kissed him. "You have the best ideas."

She walked to the bed, picked up the tiniest pair of panties he'd ever seen, then slipped them on, covering her curvy ass. Logan's feet appeared to be riveted to the floor. Now that he wanted to leave the room, he couldn't move. Elle covered her beautiful breasts with a flesh-colored bra, and then slipped on jeans and a sweatshirt big enough for them both. Her ponytail came down, and yards of brown waves spilled down her back and around her shoulders. She ran her fingers through her hair, shook her head, and then turned to him again.

"I'm ready."

"Uh," he said, trying to form words with his dry mouth. Her gaze swept across his body, pausing at the rise behind his zipper.

"But not as ready as you are." She laughed and left the room.

"You're going to get us into lots of trouble." He tried to joke away his erection to no avail.

He joined Elle, who got two bottles out of the apartment-sized refrigerator and handed him one. In a few keystrokes, she opened the email and started the download.

Her fingers trembled as she reached for her water. "I'm nervous. This could be everything I expected, or nothing."

Logan understood. "We'll know soon. The ghostwriter program should open them. But I have to warn you, if Brandon has a fail-safe built in, they will destroy themselves."

Elle rubbed her hands across her eyes. "That just can't happen. It can't."

"I hope you're right."

"Ghostwriter? It sounds very secretive." Elle pushed the laptop directly in front of Logan.

"This is a big program and will take a while to load," he said.

"Who sent the ghostwriter program?"

"Some people who require complete anonymity." Logan pulled her barstool closer. "Besides, a good cop never reveals his sources."

"Detectives and their secrets." She stroked his stubble, sending shock waves through him. "I've always loved a good mystery."

"Is that what you're reading?" Logan chuckled at her blank stare. He'd dropped his condom next to the book earlier. "The book on your nightstand? *Flirting With the Devil*?"

"Yes." She nodded. "I brought two of Kym Roberts' books with me. She's my favorite author."

"Does that one have sex in it?"

"Yes. Why?"

"Call me when you get to the sexy parts. You can read them to me."

"Stop it." She frowned up at him, but her eyes sparkled with humor. "It's about a man who's strong enough to know who he loves and is willing to fight for her."

"Smart man." Logan's stomach growled. "I'm starving."

"We just ate."

"You wore me out. I have to keep up my strength." He waited until her eyes flared and her mouth fell open. Then he kissed her and forgot he was hungry.

Digging his fingers deep into her hair, he cradled her head, holding her lips tight against his. This was no timid, bashful woman in his arms. She held her own as she thrust and parried with his tongue. When he released her, both of them were gasping for breath. Logan kissed every inch of her beautiful face and neck. He took his index finger and tipped her chin up higher. He lost himself in her gaze. Dark and smoldering, her eyes drew him back to her. Their lips met and Logan drank deep.

The computer beeped. He reluctantly pulled his mind back to the flash drive. "The program's finished loading. We'd better get busy."

Elle turned her face away from him. "Everything comes to an end."

"Not everything. This thing happening between us, whatever it is... I'm not just killing time."

"Thank you for being honest." She turned and looked him straight in the eyes. "Something is happening, and I'd like to find out what it is."

A heavy weight lifted from Logan's shoulders. "Good."

"Now, can we get some work done?" This time her sparkling eyes laughed for her.

Logan opened the folder where Elle had saved Ethridge's files and scrolled down the list. With a few keystrokes, he directed the ghostwriter program to the smallest file. "This might take a while."

"You seem to know a lot about this kind of technology."

"Oh, hell no," he admitted, hating to have her think he wasn't up on the latest. "I know people who are technology wizards. First, I ask if my particular task can be done. Most of the time the answer is yes. Then I wait for it to happen."

"Legitimate hackers—sounds like an oxymoron."

Elle's sense of humor had always been attractive to him. Brains combined with beauty made her hot as hell, which was why her brother had hovered over her like an armed drone back when they were kids.

"They're called white hats. Law enforcement keeps highly skilled technicians on the payroll. If we didn't, the whole country would be screwed."

Elle pushed her hair off her face and stared at the screen. "This has to work."

"Just remember that what we find can't be used in a court of law."

"But the more we know about Ethridge Investments, the easier it will be to use his own scam against him."

"I hope you're right," Logan said. "This step can take a long time. Let's order something off the room service menu."

"I forgot that you're hungry." She moved the room phone in front of him. "You choose."

Logan opened the room service menu, sharing it with her. "I'm having the Angus burger with cheese and bacon and a cold beer. How about you?"

"The beer sounds pretty good, but I'm going with a strawberry shake and the BLT with avocado." She scrunched up her face. "I should stick to water. Ice cream is so damn fattening."

"Order what you want." He kissed her forehead. "We'll figure out a way to work off those extra calories."

"I may have two," she said.

Logan placed their order. "ETA thirty minutes."

The program opened a file containing account information.

"You did it," she squealed like a kid at Christmas and threw her arms around him.

Logan's eyes scanned the page. "Cayman Island Bank. We may have found where he hides his money, but getting any of it back is a challenge, even for the FBI." Logan clicked on the balance tab. "Son of a bitch. There's over twelve million in this one stash. I'm betting he's smart enough to spread his money out in varying countries and banks."

"I don't recognize the name on the account." Elle pointed at the account information.

"Who is Cheyenne Forrester?" Logan clicked on account information.

"That's Brandon Ethridge's home address."

Logan growled. He retrieved his laptop and booted it up. "Let's see what we can learn about her." He entered the information in his system and started a background check.

The Internet slowed to a crawl. "Oh, my God," Elle complained. "This is as bad as dial-up."

Logan went to the curtains and drew them back. The snow was falling at a blinding pace. The landscape was covered in white. "I'll call Eric and ask him to look into Cheyenne Forrester."

"Really?" Elle's arms slid around his waist. Her cheek rested between his shoulder blades. "He'll ask about me."

"That you can be sure of."

"What will you tell him?" A touch of nerves had shadowed her words.

Logan turned in her arms. "That you are being very helpful, not taking chances, and that we've come up with a plan to make me Brandon's new target."

"That's all?"

"I'm not going to tell your brother about us over the phone. Eric deserves better." Logan leaned down and kissed the tip of her nose. "So do you."

"That's the nicest thing you've ever said to me."

"You sure? I seem to remember telling you how beautiful you looked in your pink prom dress."

"You remember that?" Her cheeks flushed pink.

"Like it was last night. Every head turned when you and Carl Winston walked in together." The memory of Elle being manhandled by that prick, flashed in Logan's mind and sent his blood boiling. "The bastard should've had his neck broken."

Elle rolled her eyes. "I should've known Eric had confided in you. Carl expected more than a just a dance. I handled the situation myself. There was no need for Eric to break Carl's nose."

Logan held back a chuckle. "That came from me. The thought that he'd put his hands on you drove me nuts."

"You?" Elle stiffened in his arms. "How did I not know this?"

"You were my best friend's sister. Eric got bent out of shape anytime I so much as looked at you."

"He had no right."

"Sure he did. We were wild as renegade wolves back then. He was only protecting you."

"Then why didn't he break Carl's nose?"

"I got to him first. In reality, I probably kept him from really getting hurt."

The knock on the door meant food had arrived. Logan signed the bill while Elle spread their feast across the coffee table.

"I didn't realize I was hungry." Elle picked up her sandwich and took a bite.

Logan grabbed his burger, and for the next few minutes, except for the occasional moan—one he decided had a different sound than the one she made during sex—silence ruled.

His cell buzzed just as he popped a french fry into his mouth. One glance at the caller ID and he shook his head. "Eric. The guy must be psychic."

Logan put the call on speaker. "I was about to contact you. Got something to write with?"

"Yeah. Why?"

"The Internet service up here is for shit. It's slow as you on the basketball court."

"If that's a challenge, I accept. What do you need?" Eric asked.

"A background check on Cheyenne Forrester." Logan spelled the name as he walked to Elle's laptop and read off the rest of the pertinent information. "There are two addresses listed, one in Fort Worth and the other in the Grand Caymans. I need everything you can dig up on her."

"And why do you need this intel?" Eric's voice lowered an octave.

Logan glanced at Elle. She rolled her eyes. Both of them recognized Eric's suspicious tone. Logan held a finger to his lips. She joined him at the bar but didn't speak.

"Brandon Ethridge has a woman with him," Logan explained. "He's presenting her as his daughter, but that's crap. I think Nicki Ethridge and Cheyenne Forrester may be the same person. So while you're at it, check out Nicki too."

"Damn it. Elle sucked you in—" Eric's voice roared through the speaker.

"That's enough," Logan snapped. Defending Elle felt right. The smile on her face confirmed it. "I think she's onto something, and I'm going to follow it through."

"I only wanted you to keep her out of trouble." The anger had faded from Eric's tone, replaced by concern. "Now I'm asking you to keep her safe."

"I'll do my best." Logan seized on a thought. "You'd have other things to worry about if you'd get off your ass and marry that girlfriend of yours."

Eric coughed. "That may be a thing of the past."

"Sorry to hear that. I thought this one had you. Email me everything you can find on both women." Logan ended the call before Eric could respond.

Elle's smile had spread wide. "Thank you."

"Not necessary." Logan turned his attention back to her laptop. "I hope we have enough download speed to operate the ghostwriter when I target one of the bigger files."

"Please, God."

"Let's try this one." Logan selected the file identified as Projects and clicked. "This will take a while."

Elle moved their dishes to the counter behind the bar. She disappeared into the bedroom and returned a minute later with her book. "I might as well get comfortable. If I don't give my brain something to do, I'll go crazy."

She tucked her feet under her and snuggled down on the couch. Logan smiled as she settled back on the pillows. The book seemed to hold her attention, but he couldn't sit still. He paced the floor, stared out the window at the snow-covered landscape, and then walked back to check on the program's progress. Elle lifted her gaze to meet his on one of his trips by the couch but quickly returned to the story, leaving him time to think.

His friendship with Eric was important. They'd been through a lot together not only as kids but also as adults. Hell, they were closer than some brothers were. How upset was he going to get when he learned his best friend was in love with his sister?

Logan stopped midstride. No, not love. Lust. Granted, this thing with Elle was different from his experiences with other women. He'd tried and failed to sustain a long-term relationship more than once. None of them had made him want permanence in his life, not like Elle did.

He checked the program's progress. He sat, drained his beer, and waited as the screen filled with color. Suddenly, everything went black except for a box in the middle of the page. It read, *Deleting.*

"Fuck." He was watching Elle's hopes vanish. He slammed his hand on the bar.

Elle jumped off the couch and ran to him. "What is it?"

* * * *

"We have to go." Brandon jumped to his feet and left Nicki sitting at the bar.

She caught up with him in the lobby and grabbed his arm. "What the hell is wrong with you?"

"Not here." He dragged his hands through his hair.

He wasn't sure which scared him the most, telling her someone might have gained access to the files or that the files had been hacked. He avoided her glare until they were safely inside their suite.

"What have you fucked up now?" she demanded.

Her blue eyes had iced over, and her cheeks were flaming red. She'd already hit her trigger. The past few days had been too good to last. "A hacker got into my computer."

"And? You notified the protection service." She poked a long red nail into his chest. "Right?"

"I did. But they haven't given me the name or IP address of the hacker yet."

"I warned you about leaving it out." She opened the mini bar and removed a scotch. "When did this happen?" She poured three fingers and tossed it down as if it were water.

"My notice came while we were skiing." He hastened to add, "I called right away. Demanded information."

"Demanded? You?"

Her laugh sent waves of nausea over him. At the same time, sexual excitement stirred low in his dick. "That's not all."

"There's more?" The smile she gave him warned of what was to come. "Do tell."

"I just received a new notice. Someone is trying to open my business records."

"Your records? Don't you mean our records?"

"Yes. That's what I meant."

"How can you be so smart at business and have no fucking common sense at the same time?" She poured another scotch and stalked across the room. "Give me your cell."

Brandon handed over his phone, careful not to look into her eyes.

"You know what to do." She grabbed his shoulders, turned him, and shoved him toward the bedroom.

Brandon heard Nicki's rant as she demanded to know exactly who was trying to violate the private files of Ethridge Investments. His worries fell off his shoulders. She would take care of things. He stripped off his clothes, opened a drawer, and removed the silk scarves he'd neatly folded and put away. He placed them and his belt at the foot of the mattress, making sure they were lined up perfectly. Then he lay face down.

Anticipation had his breath coming in rapid bursts. His cock pressed into the mattress. Had he been careless intentionally? He'd do almost anything for one session with her. His body craved the beatings. Craved the unbridled sex. Craved the discipline.

Movement above him heightened his senses, but he didn't lift his head. All his nerve endings were primed and ready. His hands and legs were secured, leaving him spread eagle, face down on the bed. The sting of the leather belt against his bare ass sent pleasure and pain rushing through him. He pressed his face deeper into the mattress to muffle his moans.

"Why must I do everything myself?" she hissed as the belt contacted his back.

Seven

"No, no, no." Elle's stomach dropped to the tops of her feet. Panic swept over her as Brandon's file disappeared. She turned to Logan. "We were afraid of this." Tears swam behind her eyes.

"Son of a bitch." Logan wrapped his arm around her. "I'm sorry."

Anger and desperation flooded Elle. She blinked hard, shoving the tears to the background. "There's information on those other files. Information we need."

He pulled her into his arms and gently rocked. "I'm sorry. This one is a total loss." She buried her face in his chest. "But don't give up on me yet."

Elle rested against him for a few seconds, drawing strength. Through the open drapes, a blanket of white weighted down the tree limbs. The branches had bowed under the pressure but hadn't broken. Neither would she. "I'll never give up."

"I still have one more method to try." He placed a call to his tech friend, explaining what had happened. Then he emailed the files to her. "If anyone can disarm the self-destruct, she can."

"That would be great. So now we wait?" Elle tried to sound as if she weren't worried. Inside, fear that she would let her grandmother down flourished.

"We do ground work." He placed his hands on her shoulders. "Go downstairs, hit the gift shop. Pretend you don't have a care in the world."

"Why? What are you going to be doing?"

"Nicki had something on her mind when she asked me to call. I'm inviting her for a drink." He leaned down for a kiss. "Maybe I can use her to get to Brandon."

"It might work. She's certainly interested in you."

"Nicki and Brandon don't know about the contest. Maybe it's time I share that tidbit with her."

Elle ignored the pang of jealousy circling around her heart. She returned to the couch and her book, covertly listening while Logan spoke with Nicki over the phone.

"She's going to meet me in the bar." Logan walked to her. He waited until she lifted her gaze and met his. "You understand this is strictly business?" His eyebrows lifted in question.

"Sure, I do." Elle returned to her reading, refusing to fall for the bait.

She watched over the top of her book while he logged off both laptops and took his to his bedroom. Elle's curiosity stirred or maybe it was jealousy. Either way, she didn't like him meeting Nicki in the bar or anywhere else. Logan didn't help matters by strolling out of his bedroom looking as if he'd stepped off the cover of *GQ*.

"Come on," he said. "It would help if you're seen out alone. Shop. Try to forget about the lost file for a couple of hours."

Elle stood and straightened his shirt collar. She dusted imaginary lint off his shirt. She didn't want him to go. After all these years of him holding her at arm's length, she wanted to take advantage of this time together.

"Do I pass inspection?"

"Stop fishing for a compliment," she joked. "You're fully aware of the effect you have on the opposite sex."

"I only care about the reaction of one individual of the opposite sex." Logan threaded his fingers through her hair and kissed her deeply. When he released her, she struggled to wipe the smile off her face.

"I gotta go."

She took his hand and walked him to the door. "Careful she doesn't wind up using you."

His laugh echoed in the hall. Quick and hearty. She loved the sound. It made his eyes dance and her knees weak as hell.

Reluctantly, she slipped on one of her new outfits, piled her hair on top of her head, and went shopping. Her first stop was the gift shop, where she purchased a pair of crescent-shaped earrings. Tiny faux diamond chips surrounded the curved blue stones. They sparkled when she moved her head and made her feel more cheerful.

Next stop was the ski shop. She spent time chatting with the ski instructor, Ryan. Tall and twenty, he had a free hour, so he suited her up and they went outside. Bundled up with nothing more than her face exposed, the cold still sent tiny prickles across her cheeks. Ryan took her through the basics and over the small manmade terrain for students.

"You don't need a lesson," Ryan said. "Too many skiers think they can hang with the more advanced, and they wind up hurt. I suggest you try the beginner slope first. If you're comfortable at the bottom, then try the more demanding slope tomorrow."

"Good advice."

After they'd gone inside, she thanked Ryan and then returned to her room, having fulfilled Logan's request. She hadn't spoken with Nan since arriving, and now would be a good time to call.

Elle kicked off her shoes, removed her bra, and piled the pillows high on her bed. With her cell in hand and her book back on the nightstand, she made herself comfortable. A call to her grandmother always made her feel better. They chatted about everything including why Elle was at Castle Alainn. She finally confided that Logan had been sent to keep her out of trouble.

"Not surprising. Eric has tried to be your dad for years. Want me to tell him to back off?"

Elle chuckled. "No. But I think Logan's going to when we return."

"It's about time. You and that boy have been mooning over each other for years," Nan said with a laugh.

"Nan," Elle answered. "What makes you say that?"

"Honey, everyone could see it but you two. Took long enough for you knuckleheads to get together."

"Could be because Eric constantly reminded Logan not to even look at me."

"That wasn't such a bad thing."

"You knew?"

"I'm old, not stupid. Last thing you or Logan needed was to have a kid at sixteen."

"You don't know that would've happened." Elle couldn't believe her ears.

Nan's sigh was a warning. She wasn't going to let Elle get away with denying anything. "Back then, neither of you had enough brains to pour piss out of a boot. Sometimes, I'm not sure about now. You are using protection, aren't you?"

"Nan," Elle exclaimed, her cheeks burning as she spoke. Silence on the other end of her call reminded her that Nan would wait until she got her answer. "Yes, ma'am."

"Good. Love happens when the time is right. But true love won't wait forever for you to catch up with it. I think you and Logan have grown up enough to handle the responsibilities that come with loving another person. You'll probably have to take control. Sometimes a man needs a little push."

"I will. He's not getting away." Elle ended the call, laid back on her bed, and stared at the ceiling. She hoped that someday she'd be as kind and understanding as her grandmother. Elle had suffered through the loss of her mom and dad, but Nan had done everything possible to fill the void their deaths had created.

Elle closed her eyes and pictured Logan telling Eric about them. Nan had been right. Elle would be forever grateful that Eric had taken on the role of protector at an early age. She hoped he'd understand and support that she was a big girl now. Sleep came easily, and Elle didn't fight it.

* * * *

Something landed on Elle's face. She couldn't breathe. Something pressed down hard on her arms and her face. She kicked her feet. Bucked her hips in desperation trying to pitch the weight off. Her lungs were going to explode. A filtered voice sounded as if it came from far away, saying something about a nosy bitch.

Darkness came even as she fought against it.

* * * *

Nicki pushed Logan's drink closer to him. She'd been distant, almost formal since arriving at the bar. They'd exchanged pleasantries, and again he'd described the bed-and-breakfast chain.' She kept glancing toward the lobby as if she expected someone.

"Are we expecting Brandon?"

"He's getting a massage. The trip down the slope was tough on him." Her gaze slid over Logan. "You took to the snow easily. Not rusty at all."

"Muscle memory." The small talk had dragged on long enough. Logan decided to push the conversation along.

"I'd better get back. The market has been all over the board. I'm thinking about dumping some stock before the price drops any further."

"You should talk to my father first." A hand on his knee startled him. "He's made lots of people rich."

Logan leaned closer and delivered his best patronizing smile. "I'm already rich."

"No one has too much money. Dad can help you stay that way." Her grip moved to his thigh.

Logan expected her to use sex as her weapon of choice, but this open display surprised him. "I've heard that before."

"No doubt," she said with a laugh. "You should give Dad a chance. At least talk to him. He has some exciting things in the works."

"I guess it never hurts to listen. But why am I sitting here with a beautiful woman talking business?"

Nicki glanced toward the lobby again. "Here's a personal question. Are you and Elle a couple?"

Finally, she'd asked the question Logan had been waiting for. He pretended to choke on his drink. "Hell no. It's a long story."

"I've got time."

Logan played it slow, making her wait. "Sounds a little goofy, but we're contest winners. It's a monthly thing here at the resort. People write an essay about why they'd like to meet someone new. The best two entries win an all-expense-paid vacation." Nicki's jaw dropped. "Before you judge me, I didn't enter. My mother, who thinks it's a crime that I haven't presented her with grandchildren, entered my name. I protested at first but then thought, why not?"

Her lips thinned. "You and Elle seemed to hit it off."

"Well, she is beautiful. I thought this might turn into a party weekend. I probably shouldn't have told her about my B and B chain. Should have kept that to myself."

"I'll just bet her little ears perked up hearing that." Nicki bared her teeth in a snarl.

"I noticed a distinct change in her demeanor."

"Money can be a burden." Nicki's shoulders relaxed. "There's something about her that makes me uncomfortable."

"She's okay. I figure everyone has an angle. Hers is finding a rich husband."

Brandon Ethridge stepped into the bar as if right on cue.

"May I join you?" Even as he asked, he was dragging a chair out.

"Of course." Logan shook Brandon's hand.

"We were just talking about you," Nicki said.

"That's true," Logan agreed.

"Logan's thinking about selling some stock. I volunteered your advice," she said.

"Did you now?" Brandon ordered a whiskey sour. "You two ready for a refill?"

"Nothing for me, thanks." Logan had already turned away three offers for more alcohol from Nicki. He wasn't falling for that.

"If you gentlemen will excuse me, I have a call to make." Nicki stood. She affectionately rubbed Logan's shoulders. "I won't be long." She kissed Brandon's cheek, then left.

"You'll have to forgive Nicki. She's always bragging about my accomplishments through my investment firm."

"You must be very proud of her," Logan said.

"For sure." His face flushed, but he recovered quickly by coughing a couple of times. "Now, if you're selling, I assume you already have a safe place to invest the money."

"Not really. My dad usually handles my investments. He's made a few bad calls, so I'm guiding the ship for now." Logan took a sip of his beer. He'd dropped the bait. Now to wait and see if Brandon bit.

"There's an investment on the horizon that could be just what you're looking for. I have a client who is looking to put together a chain of destination hotels or resorts. I'm thinking he'd be interested in adding your B and Bs."

"None of my properties are for sale." Logan pushed his chair back as if he intended to leave.

"He's also looking for a few select investors. Think about keeping your B and Bs and being part owner of a chain of resorts." Brandon's words were as practiced and smooth as the snake oil salesmen were back in the Old West. "Let's have dinner tonight. I'll bring you a packet with all the details and financials."

Logan pretended to think it over. "Let me check with Elle. I'm sure she'll want to join us."

An odd expression flashed across Brandon's face. Did he not want her to come? He hadn't heard Logan's conversation about Elle with Nicki. Not unless she'd been wearing a wire.

"Of course, I'll make reservations for four and hope you join us." The look had vanished as fast as it had formed, leaving Brandon with a forced smile. "Normally, I wouldn't consider making this offer to a stranger, but I trust Nicki's instincts. If she thinks I should give you the opportunity to double your money, then I'm game."

"I'm sure we'll see you, say, around seven?" This time Logan did stand. He shook Brandon's hand. "I'll listen to your proposition, but I'll have to know a lot more before I commit. Truthfully, it sounds too good to be true."

"Sometimes, good things happen to good people," Brandon assured Logan. He waved for the server. "The drinks are on me."

Logan kept his pace slow and easy as he meandered across the lobby. It was only after the elevator doors closed that he blew out a breath and relaxed. He almost ran down the hall to the room. He couldn't wait to tell Elle what had happened.

Alana met him at the door. Logan scanned the room. Liam stood between him and the door to Elle's room, which had been closed. Logan's gut knotted. He skipped all pleasantries. "What's wrong?"

"Elle has been attacked."

In three strides, his hand was on the doorknob.

"Wait." Alana caught his arm. "She's fine. A doctor is with her."

"What happened?" His heart rose and jammed into the back of his throat.

"Someone tried to smother her," Alana said in a whisper.

"What? My God, I should be in there with her." Anger rose from deep inside. His fingers rolled into a tight fist. He'd done a piss-poor job of taking care of her. "Why didn't you send for me?"

"I'm sorry, Logan, but she insisted you not be disturbed," Liam said.

"Disturbed?" Logan's head was going to explode.

"She called the office, and I came up straight away," Alana added quickly. "I sat with her while Liam located the doctor. She was shaken up but seemed to be okay."

"She begged me not to notify the police. I honored her request, but this makes me very uncomfortable. We're lucky that a family practitioner is here on vacation," Liam added.

"How long has he been in there?" Logan stared at the door handle.

"Maybe fifteen minutes," Alana said.

Logan dragged his hands over his face. Dozens of questions flooded his mind. The urge to pound someone to dust battled with his need to see her. The word *why* reverberated through his head.

"I'm not waiting much longer."

The door opened just as Logan finished his sentence. A middle-aged male, trim as a long-distance runner and as gray-haired as Liam, extended his hand.

"You must be Logan." The man smiled, stepped back, and waved Logan inside.

Logan wasted no time getting to Elle's side. Dropping to his knees, he leaned down into her open arms. He breathed in her scent. Ran his fingers over her skin. Her pale face and the pink hue of her eyes sent his heart into free fall. "Elle, baby. You scared me."

"Scared me too." She smiled, but her eyes hid a layer of terror.

Logan glanced up. "Doctor...?"

"Abroon." He shook Logan's hand. "She had quite a scare. The bruises on her arms and her bloodshot eyes will clear up in a few days. "You'll notify the police?" he asked Liam.

"I am the police." Logan stretched the truth since he had no jurisdiction in Colorado.

"Do you think Brandon Ethridge did this?" Alana asked.

The Fitzgeralds had no knowledge of the flash drive, so Logan was careful with his words. "I can't imagine it being anyone but him. Without proof, it's best not to accuse him."

"As soon as the roads are passable, I'll have to notify our local police," Liam said.

"Absolutely," Logan agreed.

"Then we'll leave so Elle can get some rest," Liam said.

Alana smoothed her fingers across Elle's cheek. "Call me if you need anything."

"I will," Elle said, hugging the older woman. "Thank you."

Logan escorted the trio to the door. He thanked each person individually before hurrying back to Elle. He eased down next to her and pulled her into his arms. Needing reassurance she was okay, he gently kissed her. Her warm response helped untie the knots in his gut and shifted the boulder off his chest. He ran his hands over every inch he could reach before he laid her back on her pillows.

"Do you feel like talking?"

"Yes. As soon as I get off this bed."

"You sure? The doc said you should rest."

"Then I'll rest on the couch or your bed." She swung her feet to the floor and stood. Elle leaned against him, and he led her to the common room.

Logan considered trying to preserve the crime scene but decided against it. Too many people had been in here within the past few hours. It could be days before a forensic team could get to the castle. Son of a bitch. That was why Nicki had kept looking at the door. She'd kept him busy while Brandon had tried to kill Elle.

Elle turned to Logan. "What have I started? I shouldn't have been playing detective."

Logan swept her into his arms. She buried her head in his neck as her full body shivered. He carried her into the common room, laid her on the couch, and then sat on the coffee table. He struggled to push the guilty feelings from his mind.

"We'll get through this. I'm sorry I left you alone. It won't happen again." He took her hand in his. "Close your eyes and tell me everything you remember. If you get scared, we'll stop for a while."

Elle recalled falling asleep and waking to what was probably a pillow over her face. Tears slid down her cheeks as she admitted the fear and pain she'd felt when she'd realized she wasn't able to breathe. "It was like a great weight just landed on me." She gasped. Her eyes opened wide.

"What is it?"

"I heard a voice." She closed her eyes again. "Die, you nosy bitch."

Elle's voice trembled and Logan rubbed her hand. "You're doing great. Did you recognize the voice?"

"No. It sounded so far away. I'm sorry. That's all I remember."

"Don't beat yourself up. You were wonderful. Occasionally, people can't remember anything."

"My life didn't flash in front of my face." She gave him a weak grin. "But that's when a person is drowning. Right?"

"So I've heard. What did you think about?"

"All the things I was leaving undone and words unspoken. I didn't want to die."

"There'll be time for everything." Logan refused to think about her dying. He had to concentrate on putting Brandon away for a very long time. "You make a bucket list, and I'll make sure to fulfill every wish."

"I may hold you to that." Elle pushed herself up, stood, and then took a couple of steps.

"Where are you going?" Logan asked.

"I have to move around." She stopped with one foot still in the air. "Did you move my laptop?"

"No. When I left, it was here on the counter." Logan dragged a hand across his chin. "He knows there was an attempted breach on his files and tracked it back to your laptop."

"He also must know the files self-destructed. Why try to kill me?"

"I wish I knew. That explains why Nicki was so curious about you, asking how well I knew you and if we were a couple."

"What do we do now?"

"I'll cancel dinner with the bastard. You're not going near him or Nicki." Logan wrapped his arms around Elle. Holding her as close as possible, he buried his face in her hair, imprinting her body into his memory. "Never assume. A lesson I learned years ago. Yet I assumed the bastard wasn't violent. My mistake almost got you killed."

"You can't cancel." She straightened her back and stepped away. Her dark eyes were sharp and determined. "I'm alive, and you're not to blame for the attack. Your friend needs time to break the code and send us the rest of his files."

"You can't sit across the table from the bastard after he tried to kill you. Hell, I'm not sure I can. Not without snapping his neck."

"No one but the doctor, Liam, and Alana know about the attempt to kill me, and they agreed to keep our secret."

"You think you can bluff two scam artists? It's too dangerous."

"They think you and I are almost strangers. There's no reason for them to believe you're involved with me hacking his computer."

"Damn it, Elle." Frustration boiled over. "You were almost killed."

"You think I don't know that?"

"I think you're in shock. Realization is going to hit like a tsunami. What if we're in the restaurant when it happens?"

Elle cupped his cheek, stood up on her tiptoes, and kissed him. A nice, easy, slow touch of the lips. Her tongue sought out the inside of his mouth, sweeping in and out. Jesus, she'd already figured out how to bend him to her will?

"What's the plan for dinner?" she asked.

Eight

Elle took Logan's arm as they crossed the lobby to the restaurant. She glanced up at him and smiled, remembering his expression when she'd walked into the common room wearing her ruby-red, body-hugging dress. He'd protested her plan until she'd kissed him into silence.

He stopped just short of the restaurant's entrance. "What could you possibly find funny?"

"The look on your face when you saw my dress."

"You look beautiful in it, very Christmassy. I'd like it better in a pile at your feet." His compliment was nice, but the nerves in his jaws twitched. "You're positive you want to do this?"

"Yes. It's my turn to ask if you can pull this off."

"I don't like putting you through this."

"I want to see the expression on Brandon's face when he realizes I'm alive."

Logan escorted her into the dining room. The realization that she was about to face her attacker hit her with the force of a truck. Her hands were cold as ice cubes and hung heavy at the ends of her arms. Her fight-or-flight reflexes kicked in. Her feet begged to turn toward the exit and run, but her brain demanded she pick up a wine bottle and smash Brandon in the head.

Logan's fingers found hers, sending a message of safety and support. Warmth flooded her hand, up her arm, giving Elle instant strength. She could face anybody or anything with him at her side.

Elle's gaze locked on Brandon as she and Logan arrived at the table. Brandon stood and greeted them as if they were the dearest of friends. His calm demeanor as he waited for Elle to sit shook her to the core. How much evil had to consume you before you attempted to murder a person and then pretend it had never happened?

Logan spoke first. "There's something we want to tell you, but it comes with a request that it not leave this table."

"I love intrigue," Nicki said. "I can keep a secret."

"As can I," Brandon agreed.

"Our room was broken into this afternoon. Elle was attacked." Logan's tone was flat but not confrontational. "We've asked management to keep it quiet until the pass opens and the police can be notified."

"I'm sorry to hear that. You're uninjured?" Brandon's phony look of concern sickened Elle.

She gripped Logan's knee for strength. "I'm fine." She couldn't resist turning her gaze on Brandon. She hoped he got the message that she knew what he'd done.

Logan took over and provided the couple with a brief overview, skipping the method. "It was unfortunate that Elle was in the suite when the burglary occurred," he lied.

Elle's chest swelled with pride. Logan's ability to pretend he believed that the attack on her was a burglary gone wrong was impressive.

"I should move my jewelry to the resort safe." Nicki twirled the diamond bracelet on her arm, stopped, and covered her mouth with her fingers. "I'm sorry. That sounded selfish. I'm glad you're okay."

Elle forced herself to place her hand in Nicki's. A nod was all Elle could muster. Her mind jumped around, shooting off in different directions. Neither Brandon nor Nicki displayed guilt. In fact, they both appeared to be shocked.

"Let's drop the subject," Logan said. "The only thing taken was a laptop. In a few days, we'll all go separate ways. Let's enjoy our vacation."

Elle kept a fake smile plastered on her face. At Brandon's insistence, she tried to eat, but her stomach rebelled after the first bite. Nicki asked if Elle wanted to move to the bar while the men talked business, but she declined.

Brandon handed Logan a folder filled with pictures, spreadsheets, and recommendations from people who supposedly had reaped great benefits from investing with him. Brandon went into detail about how Logan could easily double his money. The investment required a substantial buy-in, but by linking hotels, resorts, and Logan's bed-and-breakfasts under one name, the payback would be enormous and fast.

To Logan's credit, he never lost his persona of interested investor. He studied each page and asked questions. Had Elle been able to speak with him, she'd have pointed out that the entire presentation seemed strained and rushed.

After what seemed to be hours, Logan closed the folder. "It certainly appears to be a no-loss investment. But I need some time to think it over."

"I understand completely. Noble Pass should reopen soon. Nicki and I have an important client to meet in Chicago, so we'll be leaving then."

The corners of Logan's mouth lifted in a slow smile. "You wouldn't try to pressure me, would you?"

Brandon's eyes widened and he laughed. The sound reminded Elle of an old donkey her grandmother used to own. "Not at all. You can call me with your decision. Funds and contracts can be exchanged electronically."

"Sounds like a plan," Logan said, turning to her. "I have a few hours of work to do, so if you're ready."

"Of course." She dropped her napkin next to her plate.

"I'm glad you're okay." Brandon stood.

"Thank you." She swallowed the bile building in the back of her throat. "You two should join us on the slopes in the morning. We're taking it easy. I'm sticking to the beginner's course."

"I'm afraid we have to beg off," Nicki said. "I made massage appointments at the spa."

Logan's hand rested on Elle's lower back as they left the restaurant. The entire experience had wrecked her nerves. She slumped against him once the elevator doors swished closed.

"You didn't really want them to join us tomorrow."

"Oh, hell no. I wanted Brandon to believe we didn't suspect him of attacking me."

Logan had never seen this side of Elle. Her strength and bravery made his chest hurt with pride. "I've never been as proud of anyone as I am of you. You faced that bastard like the best undercover I know." He kissed the top of her head. "You didn't eat. I'll bet you'll be starving soon."

Elle turned into his arms and looked up into his dark brown eyes. How little she'd known about the man who'd captured her heart so long ago. He was strong in so many ways. Tonight he'd proven the lengths he'd go to for her.

"I'm starving." She pulled his head down and kissed him with her heart and soul. His strong arms wrapped around her, lifting her off the floor. The elevator stopped. The ding as the doors opened ended their kiss.

Logan opened the door to the suite, and she pulled him through. Her hands made quick work of his jacket and shirt. Her lips traced the muscles of his bare chest and arms.

Cool air hit her back as the zipper on her dress slid down.

"Remember what I said about that dress?"

Elle stepped back. "Hmm. Let me see." She wiggled out of the dress. It fell silently to the floor, leaving her wearing a lacy bra-and-thong combo along with her heels. "Something about liking it better off me." Her skin sizzled as his gaze swept across her body.

"Holy shit," he hissed, scooping her up in his arms.

Elle couldn't resist chuckling. "You carry me a lot."

"Get used to it." He started to her room.

"I don't want to ever get near that bed again."

"I know just the place." He turned and headed toward his side of the suite.

She nibbled the tip of his earlobe during the few short steps. He put her down, slid his hands behind her back, and unhooked her bra.

"Jesus Christ, woman, I lose track of reality when you get this close."

His words sent fire streaking through her veins. She kissed him. Hard and demanding. Her tongue surged inside, searching, teasing. His wonderful mouth chased the worries and fear of the day away. He left her lips and worked his way to the base of her jaw.

Without speaking, she slipped off her panties, took his hand, and then pulled him down onto the bed next to her. Elle traced the lines of his hard chest muscles with her tongue, placing small nips as she went. She marveled that he trembled when her fingers kneaded his flesh. Soft and hard. Smooth and strong. Her fingers crossed the ridges of his belly to the waistband of his pants. She slid the zipper down, slipped her hand inside, and found him, silky, huge, and rock hard. He thrust his hips upward, pushing his erection into her grip. His sharp intake of air was exhilarating, stoking her bravado.

"You really need to be naked."

He didn't hesitate. He made quick work of his belt and zipper, and in seconds, he lay naked next to her. He took her head in his hands and then dropped kisses across her face and neck. "You are so beautiful," he whispered into the soft spot at the base of her neck, moving down to her breasts. He pulled a nipple between his teeth, stopped, and smiled at her.

His hand pushed against her thigh, and she spread her legs, a silent plea for more. Dropping his head to her belly, he rained kisses on her trembling flesh. Working lower, he inched down her body, nipping at her flesh, before gently placing a kiss between her legs.

"Oh, God." She gasped for air. Sensations took possession of her body and mind as his tongue, warm and probing, slipped inside.

He varied his pace, sped up, slowed down, increased and decreased pressure until she thought her entire body would ignite in flames. As she tumbled over the edge, shockwaves rocketed throughout her body. She clasped her hands behind his head, holding him in place while she writhed beneath him, relishing every second of her orgasm.

He kissed his way to her stomach and then held her close until her heart slowed. Elle wanted more. "Turn over."

Logan lifted himself off her. In one swift move, they had swapped positions. She rose and straddled his hips. The desire in his eyes said all she needed to know.

"Condom." She grabbed his arm for leverage, leaned sideways to wrestle his wallet from his pants, and handed it to him.

He handed the packet to her. Heat poured from his eyes as she rolled the latex down. Elle lifted up on her knees. She took him in her hand and sank slowly down. Inch by inch, she moved until she'd impaled herself on his erection. Elle sat very still as her body adjusted to accommodate him. Desire spread through her body and begged for more. She'd jumped on a runaway train, screaming downhill, out of control.

His gaze locked on hers. "Just let go."

Logan grasped her hips, sliding her backward, then forward, up and then down. His hips rose as he thrust deep into her body. Again and again until her eyes closed, her head fell back, and she surrendered to the explosion rocketing through her body. He groaned and pulsed inside her.

Elle's heart was full as she collapsed on his chest. The words *I love you* rested on the tip of her tongue, but she held them there for only her to know. Relaxed and complete, she closed her eyes, listened as his rapid heartbeat slowed, and drifted off to sleep.

* * * *

Nicki opened the closet door. "Get dressed. Today is a big day."

Brandon crawled out, stood up, and blinked against the light. She petted his cheek, and he felt the tension drain from his shoulders. Her bad mood had passed, and the love of his life was back. Their session after dinner last night had been particularly violent. The welts on his ass would make sitting uncomfortable, but he didn't mind. He'd gotten scared and had failed to make sure Elle Reagan was dead. He had deserved the discipline.

"You, my darling," she said as she selected his clothes for the day, "are brilliant in some ways but stupid in others. Maybe that's why I love you."

"I love you too." He slid on his slacks. "Would you like me to find out if the pass is open?"

"Elle Reagan dies before we leave."

"But she didn't access my files." The minute he disagreed, he wanted his words back. He held his breath, waiting for the explosion. When none came, he breathed easier. He would pay for it later, but for now, she was calm.

"I don't know what game she's running, but it ends today."

Nine

"Hey, sleepyhead. Time to rise and shine." Logan pushed the hair off Elle's face and then leaned down to kiss the soft skin behind her ear. "It's stopped snowing and the sun is shining. I'm ordering breakfast soon."

She opened one eye, and the corners of her mouth lifted. It was enough to make his heart squeeze and his pants tighten. Her nose wiggled like a rabbit. "Do I smell coffee?"

"Yup. There's a full cup right here on the nightstand. You might have time to get in a shower before room service delivers breakfast."

"I'm up." She raised her arms over her head and stretched. The sheet slipped, exposing the most beautiful breasts he'd ever had the privilege of tasting.

"You'll be the death of me." Logan spun on his heel and headed out of the room.

"So you've said. Be careful who you give that power to."

He paused in the doorway. "I trust you with it."

"And that's a good thing." Elle raced past him, naked as the day she'd been born, to her side of the suite.

Logan ordered breakfast, then sat down at the bar. He checked his phone, hoping to find a text or message that at least one of the electronic files had been safely opened. He was also waiting for an email from Eric with information on Cheyenne Forrester. Finding neither, he opened the folder that Brandon had given him last night. Dissecting the documents line by line,

Logan looked for any claim or promise of riches. He needed facts that would hold up in a court of law.

Two hands stroked his shoulders. He'd never get tired of having Elle's hands on him or having her scent wrap around him. A knock on the door pulled him to his feet.

Minutes later, he and Elle were eating breakfast. They chatted about the weather and spending the day enjoying the beautiful mountains. It occurred to him that they sounded much like a married couple on vacation. He had to voice his concern about today.

"You weren't serious about skiing today, were you?"

"Absolutely. We're going to enjoy today. Maybe when we get back, we'll have news about the files."

He had to be honest with her. "I don't like it. Don't forget that someone tried to kill you."

"I'm not likely to let that slip my mind." Elle's head tilted to the side. "You'll be with me the entire day."

"You scared Brandon. He may not know why you're on the hunt, but he's fully aware you're nipping at his heels."

"If you're going to play the part of a rich guy, we can't hang out in the room all the time. Our free stay at the castle will be over soon. We're as safe on the slopes as we are sitting in the coffee shop. We'll be in broad daylight and surrounded by people." Elle took a sip of coffee and then stood. "I'll be ready in a flash."

Elle quickly dressed for the slopes except for her toboggan, and her heavy outerwear and boots, which were in a backpack. She'd slip them on once they got to the ski desk.

She found Logan already changed and waiting for her. He took her pack and carried it with his.

"Ready?"

She rose on her toes and kissed him. "Just remember, you're a better skier than me."

"Stronger maybe but not better." He reached for the door.

"I'll get that," she said. "Your hands are full."

She led the way to the elevator and pushed the button. Just as the doors opened, his cell chirped. He stepped inside, allowing her to enter.

Logan set the backpacks on the floor, retrieved his phone, and turned the caller ID screen toward her.

"Eric," she groaned.

Logan nodded, pushed the speaker button, and held the cell so Elle could hear. "You find something on the Forrester woman?" Logan asked.

"She's had a few brushes with the law. Three arrests for prostitution. No convictions. One of her customers filed a complaint stating that she took their role-playing too far and damn near beat him to death. He later dropped the charges. That was the last time she showed up on our radar. Where's Elle?"

Eric had changed the direction of the conversation so quickly that Logan and Elle had been caught off guard. A second of silence passed.

"She's right here. You want to speak to her?"

"No. I want you to keep her out of trouble, but do it at arm's length."

"We'll talk after I get home."

"Remember me? I know how many hearts you've left in your wake. We'll fucking talk now."

"Must've been because the right woman hadn't come along. I gotta run." Logan ended the call. "He may never forgive me."

"Sure he will. He's your best friend."

Logan stuffed his phone back into his pocket. "Interesting stuff about Nicki. That is, if she and this Cheyenne Forrester are the same woman."

* * * *

The weather outside was cold, brisk even. Elle turned her face upward toward the sun, allowing the rays to seep into her soul. The high winds of the past few days had gone away with the snow, leaving a blanket of white beauty. "The view from the top will be spectacular."

"No doubt," Logan said, helping her with her skis at the lift loading ramp. "Ready?"

The brilliance of the day, the sunlight reflecting off his sunshades, and the excitement of skiing with Logan at her side sent her into deep thought. Their future, if they were to have one, would be filled with love and laughter. She refused to think about his job and the chances he took every day. If he loved her, she could deal with the minutia. A tug snapped her back.

"This is ours." Logan helped her and then sat next to her. "You look beautiful. The sun loves your skin."

The lift lurched slightly, and soon they were rising above the ground. The higher they climbed, the more spectacular the view. As the castle grew smaller, her field of vision opened to miles of snow-covered mountains. Skiers dotted the landscape.

A quiet peace washed over her. Elle couldn't keep the truth about her feelings inside any longer.

"Logan."

A couple of popping sounds rang out. Logan jerked her to him, covering her with his body. The lift chair swung sideways and then tilted, jerking them apart. He grabbed for her, but she went flying through the air. Elle reached for him but found nothing. Her body met the snow-covered mountainside with a hard thud. White flakes flowed over her, covering her face and body. Elle pushed herself to a sitting position. Her ears rang and her back hurt like hell. Fear and worry strengthened her as adrenaline flowed through her body.

"Elle," Logan's voice boomed in the open air. "Elle."

"Here," she responded. Her panic subsided at the sound of his voice. She fell back, calmer now that Logan was making his way to her.

Logan knelt over her. Concern filled his eyes. "Are you hurt?"

"Nothing serious." She stood, grimacing at a twinge of pain in her ankle.

"We have to get out of the open. Put your arm over my shoulder. We're sitting ducks."

"So that was gunfire I heard?"

"Yeah."

Logan's eyes burned with anger as he held her close. The snow was soft powder, and his long legs pushed their way through quickly. His gaze scanned the tree line as he trudged toward the row of pines. "We'll be harder to spot." Logan stopped behind a tree and put her down.

Elle tested the ankle. "I'm fine. Nothing's broken."

Logan unzipped one of the pockets on his coat and pulled out his cell. He handed it to her. "Call Liam while I take a look around. Tell him about the gunshots and that we're about halfway up the mountain. He'll send someone to pick us up."

Elle's talk with Liam was brief. She hung up with a sigh of relief. "He'd been notified of the cable break but didn't know about the gunshots. A rescue team has already headed up the mountain." Elle kept her eyes on the horizon. "Brandon's good-old-boy routine should win an award."

"He's crazy if he thinks I won't hunt his sorry ass down." Logan, who'd been scanning the horizon, turned toward her.

Her eyes filled with panic. "You're wounded. How did I not notice that your right arm is bleeding?"

"I've had worse." He tried to ease her fear. "The bullet must have grazed a nerve. My fingers are tingling."

The roar of an engine was a welcome sound. The bright orange rescue snowmobile cruised into sight. Its driver, dressed in cold-weather gear and wearing a full-face helmet, slowed the big machine.

"Thank God." Elle pushed away from the tree she'd been leaning on, walked to the opening, and then waved. "We have an injured man. Hurry."

"Elle," Logan growled her name. He pulled her behind him, shielding her with his body. "Stay behind me."

The driver stopped and motioned for them to get on the back of the snowmobile. Logan slowly scanned the area. Elle wanted to grab him and run. If he had lost the feeling in his fingers, something was very wrong. He needed medical attention.

"Stay alert." He glanced back at her.

His troubled expression and deep frown touched her. Elle put her hand on his back as reassurance that she'd follow his instructions. It was no surprise to find that his muscles had coiled tightly.

Single file, they walked out into the open. The snow slowed their forward movement, but Logan forged ahead. A bright flash blinded Elle for a second.

The driver aimed a rifle at them. Logan whirled and pushed Elle down in the snow. Together they crawled behind a scrawny tree. He landed on top of her just as a gunshot rang out, echoing in her head.

He was trying to unzip a pocket on his right hip using his left hand. "Get my gun. Safety's on."

Elle put her hand in his pocket, feeling the cold handle in her palm. She flipped off the safety, turned to see their attacker walking toward them with the rifle aimed their direction. There was no time to give the pistol to Logan. Elle fired.

The driver stumbled backwards and collapsed.

"Stay down," Logan said. He eased up to the shooter, grabbed the gun with his good hand, and retreated as fast as possible in the snow.

"Oh, my God." Elle stared at the body. Her brain locked down as reality hit. Her chest heaved. She couldn't catch her breath. "I killed him."

"Elle?" Logan grabbed her, forcing her to look him in the eyes. "Baby. You did what you had to do."

She studied the shooter for a second longer. "Logan. Even under all those layers, I can tell that's a woman. Look at the size. That isn't a man."

Logan walked toward the body. He glanced at Elle. "I think you're right."

Elle had to know. She took a deep breath and joined him. Flashes of television shows where the killer was still alive flashed through her mind with every step. The bad guy always woke up, reached out, and grabbed the heroine's arm.

"Ready?" His eyes locked on hers.

"Yeah."

He lifted the face guard. Nicki's blue eyes stared up at them. Cold and very dead.

"You're very observant. That's the sign of a good cop. It's not too late for you to sign up for the academy."

"Thanks, but I couldn't deal with the danger."

"It was our life or hers. Never forget that."

His words had been intended to soothe and calm. She loved him for reassuring her. "Let's get you to a doctor."

"I'm okay."

"You're bleeding. Lean on me," she said.

"Have you ever driven a snowmobile?"

"I'll figure it out. Damn it, don't argue."

"Yes, ma'am." He brushed her cheek with the back of his hand. "We can wait right here."

"There's not time."

"Elle," Logan said. "I hear a snowmobile. The rescue team is coming."

Cautious and afraid, Elle slipped the pistol into her pocket but kept her finger on the trigger. After the two men removed their helmets and rushed to Logan's side, she engaged the safety.

Ten

The emergency room doctor stood back and nodded his head as if admiring his handiwork. Logan didn't care if it was pretty, he just wanted out of the emergency room. "You're cutting me loose, right?"

Elle walked through the door. "He should stay overnight."

Logan could see the stress in her eyes. She'd been through a lot in the past few hours.

"That won't be necessary. He'll be fine," the doctor said. "There's no permanent damage to the nerve. You know how it feels when you hit your funny bone and numbness spreads to your fingers?"

"Yes." Elle wiggled her fingers as if remembering that very thing happening before.

"Same feeling but times twenty," the doctor said.

"Thank you," Logan said to the doctor. Then he turned his attention to Elle.

Dark circles marred Elle's face. She had to be ready to crash. They'd been separated after arriving at the hospital. A Detective Lexington had questioned Logan first. He'd answered questions about the shooting, explained the situation to the police, and had given Eric's number for a reference. Neither he nor Elle could offer ironclad proof that Brandon knew about Nicki's plan. The detective spoke with Elle last. No doubt she'd been grilled thoroughly.

"You must be tired of answering questions."

"He just wanted to be sure we told the same story." She leaned over and kissed Logan. "I was so scared. What if you'd lost the use of your hand or fingers because of me?"

"But I didn't. I'm sorry you worried about me."

"As you should be." Her weak attempt to smile hurt his heart. Elle's eyes reflected the stress she'd been under.

The evidence backed up her claim of self-defense, but the Colorado police department had protocol to follow. The day had been hard on her. She'd come through it like a seasoned cop. Logan's pride in her grew every day. A uniformed officer and the detective on the case reentered the ER bay just as Logan slipped on his shirt. He got off the bed and caught Elle's hand.

"Detective Lexington," Logan said. "Did you have time to verify our story?"

"Yeah." The detective had yet to smile. "Can't say I appreciate the way you two handled this, but you checked out. I've stationed men at the resort to make sure Brandon Ethridge doesn't leave."

"You think he's still there?" Elle asked.

"Can't say. We had men on the scene right after the cable incident. If he left, he didn't check out. We're following up with the shuttle drivers."

"Has the word of who was killed spread?" Logan asked as he and Elle followed the detective out of the hospital.

"No name has been released."

"You checked his room?" Elle asked. "Sorry. I'm sure you did."

"Ethridge didn't respond when an officer knocked on the door. He didn't enter and conduct a search. I'm waiting for a warrant."

"If he's gone?" She smoothed a stray lock of hair off her face.

"We're watching the airport. I'm heading to the castle now." The detective turned to leave. "You two need a ride to the resort?"

Logan bargained all the way back and finally convinced Detective Lexington to let him tag along when they opened Brandon's suite.

The ride back was filled with more questions. Only this time, Detective Lexington wanted to know about possible job opportunities in Texas and the warmer climate. It seemed he had grown tired of cold weather.

Logan and Elle followed the detective into the resort, where Liam was wringing his hands and waiting for them. He quickly led them into his office, where Alana waited. She stood and walked to meet them, greeting them both with a little less enthusiasm than they'd been receiving.

"I'm glad you're both okay. Liam and I have been quite worried," Alana said. She moved to stand next to Elle.

"I'm sorry about all the trouble. It's all my fault." Elle took Alana's hand. "Neither you nor this wonderful old resort deserve bad publicity."

"Nonsense," Alana said. "We've weathered many storms. We'll come through this one. Besides, you saved us from making a bad investment."

The detective asked Liam for the card key to the Ethridge suite. Once he had it in hand, he thanked them and turned to leave, pausing to look at Elle.

"This is as far as you go. I suggest you stay here with the Fitzgeralds."

Elle marched right up to Lexington. "No. Either you take me or I'll follow. I have the most invested here. Brandon Ethridge stole my grandmother's life savings. And I was almost killed. Not to mention, I took another person's life." She glared at Lexington. "I promise to stay out of the way."

The detective had been tolerant, and Logan didn't think it wise to push him. But damn, he was proud of Elle. Her shoulders were back and her head held high. Lexington's eyes narrowed. He glared at her briefly and then sighed.

"Nothing else about this case has been by the book. You will have to stay outside the room in the hall. If I say stop, you freeze. Got it?"

"Got it." Her tone was honest, but Logan knew better. She was going to see this to the end. "If we locate him and break the news about Nicki, maybe we can get a full confession out of him. Between fraud cases from the FBI and conspiracy to commit murder from the state of Colorado, he'll be going away for a long time."

The detective stepped toward her. "You do not have control of this case."

"Of course." She nodded. "Sorry."

"Give us a minute," Logan said, walking out of Liam's office and into the lobby with Elle in tow. "This time, you need to follow instructions. Hell, the detective has been pretty damn tolerant. Don't wave a red flag in the bull's face."

She smiled up at him. "You're right."

"Wait here," the detective said, walking toward the office. "I'm going to bring a couple more men inside."

"We're not going far." Logan caught Elle's hand and led her aside. He slipped his index finger under her chin and then tipped it higher. He leaned down and kissed her, lost himself in the softness of her lips as he pulled warmth from her and fed hungrily. Her soft moan reaffirmed what he was about to do. He pushed her away from him, so she could see the seriousness of his face before he spoke.

"We don't have but a minute, and this probably isn't the time or place to say this, but I love you." He couldn't stop now. "When Eric sees how much I love you, he's going to be happy for us. And I'll make sure your grandmother never wants for anything."

"Say that again." She paled, color drained from her cheeks. "All of it?"

"No. The *I love you* part."

The knot in Logan's gut unwound. The weight on his shoulders disappeared. "I love you. Have for a long time. Will you marry me?"

Detective Lexington cleared his throat. He had two uniformed officers with him. "If you two are going, fall in."

"Yes, sir," she responded, hurrying to stay up with the men.

That she hadn't answered Logan's question was troubling.

* * * *

Elle took deep breaths during the walk to the elevator. A mixture of fear, anger, and excitement had her blood surging.

Logan dropped his arm over her shoulder. His presence instantly calmed her. She couldn't wait to spend the rest of her life with him.

"How are you holding up?"

"Good." She found she was telling the truth. "I think after it's all over, I'm going to need another vacation."

"You got it. I'll take you anywhere you want to go as long as the sand is white and the water is warm."

They got off the elevator and walked to the suite. Hanging on the door handle was the familiar Do Not Disturb sign. The detective held his finger to his lips and opened the door. He pointed at Elle, positioning her to the side. She bit back a groan but complied. The minute the detective turned his back, she moved to where she could see inside the room.

The men separated after searching the common room and walked into the bedrooms. Logan held up his hands and shook his head at her.

"This isn't good." The detective led them out of the suite. "You two check with the men at the airport. Ethridge is not to get on a plane."

Elle stood in the doorway. Her mission had been a bust. She had nothing that might recoup her grandmother's money. She turned to walk away. "Did you hear that?"

"Hear what?" the detective asked.

"Crying." She went into one of the bedrooms and listened. Whining? Elle sucked in a breath. She walked to the closet door and gently tapped.

"Nicki? Is it over?"

A hand clamped onto Elle's shoulder. Logan held his finger to his lips and shook his head. A few minutes passed.

"Did you kill her? May I come out now?"

Logan opened the door. The detective looked inside. He grabbed an oversized suitcase and tossed it across the room. What he discovered hiding behind the luggage shocked everyone. Sitting on the floor, wearing nothing but his underwear, Brandon blinked in surprise.

"Come out and meet Detective Lexington," Logan said.

In an instant, Brandon straightened his back and stood up.

"What the hell are you doing in my suite?" He blinked, then focused on Elle. "You." His jaw dropped. "Where's Nicki?"

"At the morgue by now." The detective's tone was harsh.

"No." Brandon dropped to his knees and wept like a child, sobbing uncontrollably. His muttering was impossible to understand.

What if he clammed up and the police got nothing from him? Could she convince him to talk? She had to try. Elle knelt beside him. She cringed at the red welts on his back. Softly, she whispered, "It's all over now. You'll feel better after you talk to the police."

"No. I won't. I knew we'd be caught and should've run while we could."

"Why didn't you?"

"Nicki was so sure that if she killed you, we could close the deal with Logan without anyone figuring out who shot you."

"She made you get in the closet?" Elle asked, barely holding her disgust at bay.

"Only if I did something bad. Sometimes I do stupid things and make her very angry." He started sobbing again.

"That's enough," the detective said.

Elle understood that no one had read him his rights, so she reluctantly stopped talking. A uniformed officer came, lifted Brandon to his feet. While the detective mirandized Brandon, he put on his pants, a shirt, and shoes. Then an officer handcuffed Brandon.

Relief washed over her in waves.

"Who killed Nicki?" he asked.

"I did," Elle said.

The detective looked at her and then at Logan. "You'll have to stick around for a few more days. I'll get you back to Texas before Christmas. You might have to come back for the trial, but I have a feeling Mr. Ethridge is going to be very forthcoming."

Logan and Elle stayed with Detective Lexington, his men, and his prisoner until Brandon was loaded into the back of a police car and hauled away from the castle.

"You know what I'd like?" She leaned into Logan, taking time to enjoy the beautiful day.

"Me?" His arm slipped around her waist, pulling her closer.

"You're wearing a sling. I'm not making your injury worse. I was thinking about another strawberry shake."

Logan snuggled her against him. "I can take this sling off, but you'll have to be gentle with me."

She laughed at his joke. This trip had far surpassed her expectations. Maybe her grandmother had been right. Love happens when the time is right.

Eleven

Elle helped Nan put a couple of bows on the Christmas tree. Not that she needed help. Nan had already hung every decoration that Elle and Eric had made, along with bulbs, bows, lights, and tinsel. She'd been given the job because her pacing had gotten on her grandmother's nerves.

"It's beautiful," Elle said as she backed across the room. "What's in the big box?"

"None of your business." Nan moved to stand between Elle and the present under the tree. "You'll have to wait until Christmas morning."

Elle heard a noise. Logan had dropped her off at Nan's before he joined Eric for lunch. Elle had wanted to go and voice her opinion, but Logan had won the argument. This was something he wanted to do alone. "Logan's back."

"I didn't hear anything," Nan said with a chuckle. "He's taking care of business. Relax."

Elle walked to the front door and looked out. It was nothing. "I should have gone with him. You think he and Eric are arguing?"

"No way of knowing. My money is on Logan." Nan pushed the screen door open. "He's only been gone a couple of hours. Come sit in the porch swing next to me."

Elle followed Nan outside but paced the length of the porch instead of sitting.

Another thirty minutes passed before Elle spotted the dust rolling off the dirt road that led to Nan's house. "Finally."

Logan parked his pickup and got out. He straightened his shirt, walked up the drive and down the sidewalk without changing expression.

"I knew it." Elle turned to Nan. "Eric hates the idea of me and Logan in love."

"I don't believe it," Nan said.

Elle ran to meet him at the yard gate, lifting up on her toes for a kiss. Logan leaned down, brushing her lips with his. Nan waited for them on the steps.

"Afternoon, beautiful," he said, turning on the charm for Nan. He smiled at her, and the Texas sun got brighter.

"Good to see you." Nan turned her cheek for a kiss. "It sure felt like you and Elle were gone a long time."

"But we made it back in time for Christmas."

His mood was too good. Nan had been right not to fall for his solemn look. He was just making them wait.

Nan huffed. "Good thing you did."

Logan sniffed the air. "I smell blueberries, which means a cobbler just came out of the oven."

"I was just going in to take it out of the oven. Your timing is perfect." Nan squinted, looking him over from top to bottom. "I don't see any bruises."

"No, ma'am. Eric took it a lot better than I expected." Logan slid his arm around Elle's waist.

"Told you it was right to let him go alone," Nan said, enjoying the fact that she'd been right. "In five minutes, I'm dishing up vanilla ice cream to top off my cobbler. Any takers?"

"We'll be right in," Elle said, holding onto Logan's arm. She waited until the front door closed. "You scared the crap out of me. What did Eric say?"

"Something about me damn near getting you killed."

"Really?" Elle pulled Logan down to the porch swing. "I thought you said it went okay."

"It did. I was joking."

She smacked him in the stomach. "Give me details. What did he say when you told him we were getting married?"

"Are we?" His eyebrows lifted in question. Was he joking again?

"You proposed. And you're not taking it back!"

"Can't take something back that was never accepted."

"I said yes." Her mind raced back to that day in the castle's lobby. "Didn't I?"

"Nope. You never answered my question."

"Then do it again." Her heart was about to explode. "Stop teasing and say it again."

"I made one other stop before I came back." Logan removed a small box from his pocket and opened it to reveal a beautiful engagement ring. "Will you marry me?"

"Yes. Yes. Yes." She kissed him, putting her heart and soul into the kiss.

"Merry Christmas," he said.

"It's beautiful." Tears flooded her eyes as he placed the ring on her finger. The winter wind lifted her hair, reminding her how nice it was to be back in Texas. "I'm so glad we made it home before Christmas."

The front door opened. "If that's settled," Nan said with a grin, "cobbler's getting cold."

Author's Note

I'd love for you to check out the other Noble Pass Affaire titles by members of Chick Swagger, listed in the front of this book—here's a sneak peek at *Flirting with the Devil* by Kym Roberts:

Flirting with the Devil

"Do you remember anything about last night?" He pushed again. Praying that she remembered.

Looking down at her feet, she replied, "I remember what you walked in on...did Ty do that to your lip?"

He only gave her half an answer, "No, there was an unruly passenger at the airport."

She waited for more, but they'd been here, done that with the other part of her question. It was not a memory he wanted to dwell on, and yet at the same time, Wade's heart nearly broke in half.

She didn't remember any of it.

"Was it real? Last night?" she asked.

That hope just kept knocking on his heart, dying to get in. "It was more real than the nightmare I've been living since the day you left."

"Did we sleep together?"

With all of his being, he wished they had. It'd been so long. "We slept together, yes." Her eyes shot up at his face and he smiled. "That's all we did. We didn't have sex."

"Oh."

Again, that hint of disappointment that gave him so much hope he wasn't sure what to do with it. Until she asked, "Why are you here?"

He knew why he was there. He loved her. More than anything, and he damn sure didn't want to lose her ever again.

But he didn't have her. Not yet, anyway. Last night, at her weakest, most vulnerable moment, she'd trusted him.

Today, she wasn't sure where to turn—to trust in the lie of the past six months, to believe the lessons from her past that told her love was a myth—or to side with the truth and the devotion from the man standing in front of her. The man she loved with all of her being. He now understood, more than ever, the battle she faced.

Half of it had nothing to do with him and everything to do with a dead mother and a father who'd left her, at the age of nine, in a homeless camp made of boxes. Frightened and alone. Shivering from the cold, dressed in clothes five sizes too big that had belonged to her mother.

But could she really trust a member of the human race with her heart? Unconditionally? He'd thought she had learned how—with him. But the past six months had erased everything.

Knowing her childhood, he wasn't sure he could win. Especially when she was afraid to trust...to feel.

She searched his eyes for the truth, and he prayed she could read it. Feel it in his touch.

"I thought that Ty was the better man for you. He has the training, the skills, everything it takes to keep you safe. I build houses..." He laughed and looked away. He never would have believed he'd be embarrassed by owning one of the premiere building corporations on South Carolina's seaboard. He and Reese built dream homes. They were featured on television for their vision and design. Yet he couldn't protect his wife...from the mob.

"That wasn't your fault..."

"Wasn't my fault?" He couldn't believe she was letting him off the hook. "If I had been there with you to celebrate your victory, that scumbag wouldn't have gotten within two feet of you."

"He would have killed you first. Put that blade in your back without us ever seeing him. You wouldn't have stopped the attack on my life. It would have left you dead, and I would have had to go on living knowing that I was the reason for your death."

"Would you have cared?" He knew the answer. She loved him, but he needed her to admit it to herself.

And she did, with indignation that he would ever doubt her feelings. "Of course I would care!" Her voice grew softer, "You're the only person I've ever loved in my life."

He seized the moment. "Give us another chance, Sam. You know I didn't cheat on you. I would never risk losing the woman who made me complete, not for a meaningless affair, not for my company, not for anyone or anything. I found love when I met you. The moment you fell into my arms, I knew you were the one for me." His voice hitched with emotion before he looked her in the eyes and put everything on the line. "The only one for me."

"Your miniskirt with the zippers on each side about drove me crazy. I wanted to unzip it with my teeth, unravel the present that had dropped in my arms and gave my life meaning. I'd thought I was happy, before I met you. But I wasn't..."

She was staring at him like she couldn't believe he remembered what she'd been wearing that fall day. But he did. From her tight jean skirt to her black sequin top and short black boots. She'd been his fantasy in the flesh that day. Just like today.

"Your hair was up in a clip, and just as you fell into my arms, the clip slipped and your hair tumbled out. It was like sheets of black satin unfolding in my arms."

She reached up and put her finger on his lip, searched his face for the truth of his love, as if she was remembering the moment when he'd held her in his arms for the very first time. Six years ago, the desire to kiss her had been so strong he didn't think he'd be able to resist. But he had. Because their future was on the line.

Today, however, was a different story. Holding back the passion would be all wrong, and he knew it. Knew she needed to be reminded of how good they were together. It was now or never.

Enfolding her in his arms, he dipped her backwards like the day they'd met. But this time he didn't resist the sweet temptation inches from his mouth. "This is what I wanted to do the day we met."

His lips touched hers ever so gently, waiting for her to respond, to give permission for him to take it further. With a little sigh, her arms encircled his neck, and he was done resisting. Done holding back the passion and need that this woman created within him. His mouth devoured what she gave. And oh, how she gave.

Until she stopped.

With tears in her eyes, she buried his hopes. "I can't do this."

Unedited excerpt: No Greater Hell

Jake settled his ball cap on his head to shade his eyes against the morning sunlight. He blinked against the glare as he scanned the Donovan Ranch for damages. His joints were stiff, more from tension than being cramped underground in a storm cellar for the past six hours. Neither he nor Aunt Alice had slept, not with the torrential rainfall and high winds pounding against the only door out of this underground shelter.

A battery powered weather radio had kept them up to date on the deadly hurricane that hit the coast of Texas. It had spawned three tornados and dumped untold inches of rain. He and Alice had known exactly when the tornado had passed over the ranch. The past few days the two of them had worked nonstop. Alice had already proven that she could carry her weight. She'd boarded up windows, stacked furniture, and moved food to the cellar while Logan had moved the cattle and then the horses to higher ground. Strong and determined, she'd worked harder than any two men. His level of respect and affection grew every day.

It was quiet now. The air was still. Even the birds had stopped chirping. Probably too scared to announce the danger had passed. Alice stood silently beside him. Her blue eyes looked permanently stained with red streaks from the lack of sleep. Her salt-and-pepper hair mussed from lack of care, not that she cared.

"Thank God the house is still standing," she said. "Roof looks to have shingles missing over the back bedroom." She pulled an old ball cap from her hip pocket and socked it on her head. "Damn twister cut a swath right through the pasture. I'll take a look at the house. You'll check on cattle and horses?

"Yes ma'am." Jake had no words of comfort to offer. Nothing he could say would make things better.

He escorted his aunt to the front porch then went to the barn, surveying damage as he walked. Rapidly moving water had cut a wide swath in the usually hard dirt road from the house to the out-buildings. Uprooted paddock fence posts, felled young trees with their jagged roots pointing skyward, which would've someday provided the livestock shade from the broiling Texas sun, dotted the pasture. The odor of wet wood and soggy cattle pens went unnoticed as he pulled on a tall pair of rubber boots. The four-wheeler would get stuck, so he walked. His feet sinking into the mud with each step.

Within a few hours, Jake had located the livestock and counted four dead. He stared in amazement at a new born calf and her mother. He gathered the heifer in his arms, knowing the mother would follow, and carried it back to the barn. Secure in a horse stall with a fresh pile of hay, both animals would be fine.

Jake tugged off the rubber waders, dropping them on the back porch steps. He turned on the water hose and rinsed them off followed by his face, arms, and hands. The heat and humidity had taken their toll on him, soaking his clothes clean through.

Alice opened the door and handed him a towel. "If you'd let me cut off about four inches of that hair, you'd stay a lot cooler."

"You're probably right." He laughed and brushed off her comment. It had been a long running joke, starting the minute his hair got long enough to brush the tops of his ears.

"How'd the livestock look?"

"Better than expected. Many trees in the upper forty were uprooted. We fared better in the small pasture on the hill. Not near the damage up there as the low land. "He handed the towel back.

"The roof held better than I expected, she said. "I didn't find any leaks."

I'll get up there and tack down tarp. That will have to do until I can get replacement shingles."

"That can wait. The power's out and the ice won't last long. I made a jar of sweet tea. It's instant but it will have to do. Come set for a minute. I'll pour you a glass."

"I'm fine. I'll get something to drink after while."

"Now don't be arguing. I need you inside for a minute."

Jake followed the fifty-five-year old, tough as nails, woman rancher into the house. She was an attractive woman with short salt and pepper hair and a clean and healthy glow about her. They'd worked hard to keep the ranch going after his uncle Charlie died. Her last vestige of fight seemed to have died when she walked out of the storm shelter and saw the aftermath of the storm.

"I'll pour," he insisted, taking the tea jar from her. He glanced up at the ceiling. "We got lucky."

"That we did. This old house held together better than I expected." Alice picked up her cell. "I pulled up the weather. We're a heck of a lot better off than the cities and cattle ranchers closer to the coast. Connersville caught the worst of the tornadoes. Lots of people without power. A few families lost their homes."

Jake hated the sadness in her voice. He had something sure to cheer her up."I brought you something."

"You did?"

"Drink your tea. Then we'll walk down to the barn."

Her eyes brightened a little. "You didn't find a calf?

"Yep. I put her and her mama in the back stall. The ground is soggy, but I spread out a couple of bales of hay. They're both going to be fine."

Jake heard a vehicle drive up outside. He stood and walked to the door. "The sheriff is here."

"That's why I wanted you to come inside. He called. Wants to talk to you."

Also By Jerrie Alexander

Romantic Suspense
    The Green-Eyed Doll
    The Last Execution
    Hell or High Water
    Cold Day in Hell
    No Chance in Hell
    No Greater Hell
    A Helluva Holiday
    Till Justice is Served
    Till the Dead Speak
    Someone To Watch Over Me
    Flirting With Fate
    Skyway to Hell – coming soon
    Contemporary Erotic Romance
    Come Hard
    Come Hot
    Come Together
    Come Undone

About the Author

I live in Texas with my rescue dog, Hazel. I write about alpha males and kick-ass women who weave their way through death and fear to emerge stronger because of, and on occasion in spite of, their love for each other.

If you enjoyed this novella or any of my books, please help me spread the word. Facebook and tweet your approval. A review on Amazon, Barnes & Noble, and Goodreads would be greatly appreciated. Send me an email if you post a review, I'd love to thank you personally.

Get up-to-date information on new releases. Connect with me on Facebook[1] and Twitter[2].

---

1. https://www.facebook.com/pages/Jerrie-Alexander%20/
121521571355959?ref=hl

2. http://www.twitter.com/jerriealexander